Paul Wenz was born in 1869 into a wealthy French wool-buying family. He first visited Australia in 1892 and decided to settle in New South Wales in 1898. He married an Australian, Harriet Dunne, and took up a large property on the Lachlan River between Forbes and Cowra. Before the First World War he published a number of short stories written in French and set mostly in Australia; in 1908 his only work written in English, *Diary of a New Chum*, was published in Melbourne. He visited Europe regularly and served as a liaison officer in France during the war. From 1919 to 1931 he published four novels, some memoirs and more short stories, all of which were published in Paris. He became more involved in Australian literary life during this period, but because he wrote in French he remained unknown to all but a few until his death in Forbes in 1939.

Maurice Blackman was Head of the Department of French at the University of New South Wales. He was also director of the French-Australian Research Centre at the university. Dr Blackman has also published in the area of modern French literature, including *Diary of a New Chum* and *The Thorn in the Flesh*, both by Paul Wenz.

OTHER BOOKS IN THE
SYDNEY-PARIS LINK SERIES:

A
Coral
Eden

PAUL WENZ

Introduced and translated by Maurice Blackman

ETT IMPRINT
SYDNEY-PARIS LINK

First published by ETT Imprint, Exile Bay in 2021

First published as *Le Jardin des Coraux* by Calmann-Levy, 1929

ETT Imprint
PO Box R1906
Royal Exchange NSW 1225
Australia

ISBN 978-1-922473-83-7 (pback)
ISBN 978-1-922473-84-4 (ebook)

A Sydney-Paris Link publication
In memory of Jean-Paul Delamotte

Cover: Fish and coral. Photographer Frank Hurley
Courtesy Australian Museum Archives AMS320/vv3243
Cover design and internals by Tom Thompson

CONTENTS

Hettie and Paul Wenz with Miles Franklin (at right), Nanima 1937.

PAUL WENZ:
LIFE AND TRAVELS

by Maurice Blackman

Paul Wenz was born on 18 August 1869 into a wealthy French Protestant family of German origin. His father was well established in the wool trade, and owned woollen mills in Reims; the family company imported wool from South America and Australia. Paul was the third of five children, with two older brothers and a younger brother and sister.

At the age of ten Paul was sent off to a private school in Paris, the Ecole Alsacienne, where he seems to have had an average career, although he was reportedly good at written composition. During his school years he befriended fellow pupil André Gide: this friendship would be reactivated in later years, and Gide would become a helpful supporter in Wenz's literary activities. Another friend was Joseph Krug, of the famous champagne family.

After leaving school and performing his compulsory military service, Wenz had a brief initiation into the family business, and was sent off to London for the best part of a year to learn English, and presumably to find out more about the wool-importing trade. Wenz's eldest brother, Emile, had travelled in Australia and New Zealand in 1884 to visit the agents and offices of the family-owned wool-broking agency Wenz & Co. which had established branches in Sydney and Melbourne in 1879. (The agency was quickly successful, and remained a force in the wool trade until the end of the 1970s.) Wenz was impressed with his brother's travel tales when he returned.

Paul Wenz was an active, outgoing young man who had a hearty appetite for travel and the outdoor life – it was an appetite that he would maintain until the end of his days. At the beginning of 1891 he set off to Algeria to try his hand at wine-growing, but after a year of problems, he decided against Algeria. On the advice of his father and eldest brother, Paul set sail for Hobart and Melbourne, where he arrived in October 1892. He seems to have liked the country immediately, and he spent the next three years jackerooing in Victoria, New South Wales and Qeensland. He also managed to visit New Caledonia and several islands in the South Pacific. In 1896 he spent several months in New Zealand and visited some estancias in Argentina and Uruguay. He returned to France in September 1896.

Back in France, he announced to his family his decision to settle permanently in Australia as a grazier and immediately began arrangements to emigrate. It was perhaps on the boat bringing him back to Australia in 1897 that he met and fell in love with a young woman of his own age, Harriet Dunne, daughter of a wealthy grazier from Melbourne and Netley Station (near Menindie in New South Wales); they became engaged soon after his arrival. At the end of 1897 he purchased a large sheep and cattle station called Nanima on the Lachlan River, about halfway between Forbes and Cowra, in some of the best sheep-raising country in New South Wales. He married Harriet ('Hettie') Dunne in September 1898, and had a large residence built on his new property.

With Harriet's help, Wenz prospered as a grazier and made many improvements to Nanima, including the installation of an advanced irrigation system, but he already had other ambitions: he began writing short stories, written in French but set mostly in Australia. The first of these appeared in 1900 in a Paris magazine called *L'Illustration* under the pseudonym 'Paul Warrego', a name he would go on using for several years. In the early years of the new century *L'Illustration* would publish a number of Wenz's stories, most of which had Australian bush settings, although some were also set on South Pacific islands. These early stories brought to life for a French public the typical characters of the Australian bush. Wenz was very impressed with the hardy nature and stoic humour of Australian rural types, and also with the independent spirit of the new Australian Federation. He respected the harshness and strange beauty of the bush, and appreciated the experience of bush life.

His first stories found a receptive audience in France, which was already curious about the newly emerging nation, and in 1905 Wenz published a collection of sixteen stories entitled *A l'autre bout du monde (At the Other End of the World)* under his pen-name 'Paul Warrego'; it ran to a second edition in 1907. Wenz and his wife sailed to France for a long visit in 1905, and he was able to renew contact with his family and his old friend Joseph Krug.

On his return to Australia, via the United States, he began work on his first and only book to be written in English: *Diary of a New Chum* was published in Melbourne in 1908 (new edition published by ETT Imprint, 1990 and 2021) again under the pen-name 'Paul Warrego'. At the end of 1908 the Wenzes met and became good friends with the American author Jack London and his wife Charmian, who were then staying in Sydney. Doubtless as a result of this friendship, Wenz undertook to translate into French one of London's books, *Love of Life*.

Wenz and his wife loved to travel, and they set off for France again in 1909, this time travelling through South-East Asia and China, thence by Trans-Siberian Railway to Europe. During their long stay in Europe, Wenz renewed his acquaintance with André Gide, who was by now an author of some note. Wenz introduced Gide to the work of Jack London and discussed the possibility of publishing his proposed translation. The Wenzes returned to Australia in 1910, and that same year there appeared in Paris a second collection of short stories, *Sous la Croix du Sud (Beneath the Southern Cross)*, this time published under Wenz's own name. Again, the stories mostly have bush settings, with a few set on Pacific islands, and once more the collection ran to a second edition in 1911. In 1912 Wenz sent the completed manuscript of his translation of *Love of Life* to Gide, and the work was published with great success.

After more travels, this time in South America, and another long stay in France, Wenz and his wife were caught in Reims at the outbreak of war in 1914: they endured the catastrophic bombardment of Reims, including the destruction of the Wenz family home, and decided to stay on. Wenz became a liaison officer in the Franco-British military hospital while Hettie worked for the Red Cross. In 1915 Wenz was transferred to London as a liaison officer with the Red Cross, and after Australian troops were posted to France in 1916, he had regular contact with Australian personnel, both on his regular visits to France and with Australian troops recuperating in England.

In 1915 Wenz's first novel, *L'Homme du soleil couchant (The Sundowner)*, which he had written before he left Australia, appeared in serial form in the *Revue de Paris*. After 1916 Wenz published in several French magazines stories based on his experiences as liaison officer with the Red Cross and wrote a second novel, *Le Pays de leurs pères (Their Fathers' Land*, translation published by ETT Imprint, 2018), about Australian soldiers on leave in England, which was also serialised in the *Revue de Paris*. Back in France at the beginning of 1919 Wenz published two small collections of wartime stories set in France and England. In the same year *Le Pays de leurs pères* appeared as a book: although it was his second novel, it was the first to be published in book form. In April 1919, Wenz travelled through Morocco as liaison officer and translator with a special Australian agriculture and trade mission to the French Protectorate.

The Wenzes returned to Australia in November 1919 after an absence of more than six years, and Wenz resumed his life as a grazier with some gusto, apparently putting aside writing for the time being. A few stories, with English or French settings, appeared in the early 1920s, but they had most likely been written while Wenz was still in Europe; *L'Homme du soleil couchant* was published as a book in 1923, but that had been written nearly ten years before.

The Wenzes still had their hearty appetite for overseas travel, and set off once again for Europe in April 1924. While in France, Paul arranged the publication of a short guide he had written on Australian sheep-raising methods. He was also engaged to undertake an official mission to report on sheep and wool production in the French West African colonies. Paul and Hettie set off on their adventurous mission at the beginning of March 1925, travelling by car, train and river barge through Senegal, Mauretania, Niger and Ivory Coast, and making a special visit to the fabled city of Timbuktu. In early May they sailed from Dakar to the Canary Islands, where they spent a month recuperating from the rigours of their African journey, and in early June they departed from Teneriffe by boat for Capetown on their way home to Australia. During their voyage they spent a day visiting the isolated island of St Helena, site of Napoleon Bonaparte's final exile, and after their arrival in Capetown they went on a four-week tour through South Africa and

Rhodesia. They finally arrived back in Sydney towards the end of August.

In June 1927 they set off once again for Europe, sailing via South-East Asia, Saigon and Colombo to Marseille; they spent most of 1928 staying on the French Riviera, with occasional visits to friends and family. Paul Wenz probably undertook some more writing during this stay, and he would have arranged for the publication of one or more of the books that were to appear at the end of the decade. Paul and Hettie set sail from France in February 1929, this time accompanied by Paul's widowed sister Aline and his niece Alice. They disembarked in Fremantle in early March and took the newly completed Transcontinental Railway from Perth to Sydney (a journey of three days and three nights); Aline and Alice would stay at Nanima for five months.

In 1929, 1930 and 1931 three books by Wenz appeared in succession: *Le Jardin des Coraux (A Coral Eden)*, a novel set in Sydney and on the Barrier Reef, *Il était une fois un gosse (There Was Once a Silly Kid)*, a book of fanciful childhood memoirs, and *L'Echarde (The Thorn in the Flesh*, translation published by ETT Imprint, 2004 and 2018), a novel set in South Australia. Also dating from the early 1930s are a number of mostly unpublished manuscripts – a book of travel memoirs, a group of Arabian Nights-style tales, another group of light-hearted stories for children (written for the children of his nieces and nephews in France: he and Hettie had no children of their own), and a few more Australian bush stories.

Wenz's fortunes do not seem to have been greatly affected by the Great Depression of the early 1930s, but he does complain about the occasional drought or flood, and he is pessimistic about New South Wales politics. At the end of June 1932, the Wenzes sailed once again from Sydney to France for their regular visits to friends and family. In February 1933 they went to Lisbon to take a cruise across the Atlantic to Brazil, and up to Manaos, 1600 kilometres up the Amazon; they were back in France at the end of March. In June they spent several weeks in London, and then took a month-long motoring holiday through Scotland. They returned to France in mid August and sailed for Sydney at the beginning of October, with a brief stopover in Colombo.

For the next few years Wenz spent most of his time at Nanima. He and Hettie took a long cruise to the Whitsunday Islands in May-June 1935, spending three weeks on West Molle Island, and Paul made a short trip to New Zealand in March-April 1936. He continued to write during these years, mostly short stories, and even published a few travel articles and other journalistic items in magazines. He also engaged more actively with literary colleagues in Australia and with the Australian literary scene in general. It was not until January 1938 that Paul and Hettie set out on another major voyage. This time they sailed across the Pacific via Tahiti and the Panama Canal to visit the French Caribbean islands, and arrived at Marseille in March. Once again they spent time on the French Riviera and made family visits; they also attended French-Australian memorial ceremonies at Villers-Bretonneux in July. Paul seems to have spent the rest of the year approaching various publishers and editors about possible publications. However, he had no success with these approaches, and at the end of March 1939 the Wenzes left France to return to Sydney.

After this final trip to England and France Wenz returned to Nanima in May and fell ill with pneumonia in July; he died in Forbes Hospital from complications on 23 August 1939 at the age of 70, and is buried in the Forbes cemetery. His wife Harriet stayed on at Nanima until 1949, when she retired to Manly, and died there in 1959. She is buried with Paul Wenz in the Forbes cemetery.

PAUL WENZ'S AUSTRALIA

As we have seen above, Wenz had a love of travel and adventure; he also had the resources to travel as much as he liked. After he arrived in Australia, he spent his first few years working and exploring in Tasmania, Victoria, New South Wales and Queensland. While he was in Queensland, he took the opportunity to visit the Great Barrier Reef and several Pacific islands. At the beginning of 1895 he spent some time in New Caledonia, and probably also visited the Solomon Islands, New Hebrides (now Vanuatu), Tonga, Samoa and Fiji, travelling on small trading ships between Queensland ports and the islands. He had an interest in French maritime history, and particularly in the voyage of La Perouse, his explorations of the Pacific and his sojourn in Australia. He would have visited Vanikoro in the Solomons, which was the site of the wreck of La Perouse's two ships in 1788. In August 1895, in Far North Queensland, he spent some time at a site on the coast north of Mackay where wreckage had been found that was thought to have belonged to a boat that had perhaps brought over some survivors from the shipwreck at Vanikoro.

Wenz's first published book, *A l'autre bout du monde* (1905) is a collection of sixteen short stories. Eleven of them are set in Australia, mostly in the bush, and five take place on Pacific islands or at sea. Two of these are of interest in relation to this present novel: '*En Nouvelle-Calédonie*' ('In New Caledonia') is a tale of colonial vengeance between an immigrant worker and a French official; '*Une soirée à Tonga*' ('One Evening in Tonga') gives a picture of life on that island. A third story is also interesting: '*L'évadé*' ('The Escapee') is set in a lighthouse on the North Queensland coast; the lighthouse crew encounter an escaped political prisoner from New Caledonia. In these stories we can see a kind of premonition of some of the elements in *A Coral Eden*.

When he returned to Australia after his long absence in Europe, Wenz seems to have undergone a change in his relationship with the country. In his pre-war writing, he is the amused observer and interpreter of Australian life and ways for a curious French audience. He is firmly in the camp of the Bulletin writers who see bush values as the essential Australian values, and he contributes to the saga of the development of a surprising new nation. After his war experiences and contacts with Australians serving in France, he takes a more accepting, even celebratory view of the Australian character and seems to be identifying more with Australia, going further in his psychological analysis, even if he maintains a gently ironic stance. He also seems at this time to be starting to identify as an Australian writer, even if he is writing and publishing in French. He cultivates correspondence and friendship with Australian literary figures, tries to promote translations of his works in Australia, and participates more actively in Australian literary life. He also begins to explore regional Australia again, this time with the motor car.

There is also a reorientation in the themes of his novels and stories. Whereas the pre-war stories deal primarily with the difficulties and small triumphs of conquering and settling a new nation and are almost all set in "the bush", two of the novels he wrote in the 1920s have modern urban settings, even if these are contrasted with nostalgia for a past version of colonial Australia, or with an idealistic yearning for a paradise in nature. *Le pays de leurs pères* deals with Australian soldiers on leave or recuperating in London during World War 1. In their different ways, the soldiers confront the differences between the modern city of London and their previous lives in colonial Australia. These contrasts lead to a certain readjustment, perhaps even a maturity, of their attitudes towards both Britain and Australia. *Le Jardin des Coraux (A Coral Eden)* begins with a lively, bustling depiction of a modern Sydney that is definitely part of the wider modern world, with all its flaws and advantages. In one chapter, there is even a comparison between the liveliness of Sydney and the dreary stuffiness of London. The two central figures in the novel are young, vital urbanites, rather than stock outback characters, who try to live out an idealistic escape into a tropical paradise. Even if their ideals end up being crushed, the initial impetus of the story is forward-looking and full of enthusiasm.

Le Jardin des Coraux and his final novel *L'Echarde* are his most ambitious works. While *L'Echarde* casts a final look back at the bush world of his earlier writings, it shares with *Le Jardin des Coraux* a more sophisticated narrative structure and a stronger psychological interest in character. They are more dramatic than his previous novels, and they both have a more fatalistic progression towards a tragic climax. Indeed, *Le Jardin des Coraux* made enough of an impact in France to prompt a film producer to approach Wenz in 1934 with an offer to turn it into a film. (Unfortunately, nothing ultimately came of this proposal.) Formally and thematically, they are his most successfully realised novels, and together they give a complete representation of the themes and characters that make up Wenz's literary world.

A CORAL EDEN

In many ways, this is arguably Wenz's best novel. Although his other works have a definite nostalgic charm, this novel, with its urban setting, younger characters, swiftly moving plot and complex psychological exploration, strikes us as being much more modern. We can perhaps even see Wenz making some modernistic moves with occasional passages of stream-of-consciousness and subjective point of view. Be that as it may, the themes of the novel have a certain contemporary flavour: a youthful enthusiasm to travel and take on the modern world, the desire to create one's own world and launch oneself into new experiences, coupled with a certain disillusion with aspects of modern life and the urge towards a better accommodation with the world of nature, these still have resonance a century after Wenz composed his novel.

The period he chooses is interesting. The modern urban setting, with its energy and optimism, has not yet collided with the disaster and disillusionment of the First World War. We seem to be in about 1910, with a booming economy and an outward-looking population. Certain passing references in the text – the presence of Jack London and his boat in Sydney and the names of certain ocean liners for instance – connect us with some of Wenz's own experiences at that time, as well as opening the story up to the world outside Australia. It is clear that Wenz works many elements of his own travels into the narrative. There are certainly traces of his own observations and memories from his first explorations of Queensland and the islands of the South Pacific. We know that he took further cruises and voyages in and across the Pacific in the 1930s; perhaps he also had some trips to Queensland and the Barrier Reef in the 1920s as well. Tourism was certainly beginning to develop in Queensland at that period, with the first resorts starting to appear on the coastline and some of the islands in the Coral Sea. Publicity for tourism was also booming with the advent of new magazines, in particular a lavishly illustrated travel magazine called *Walkabout*, which was popular up until the 1960s.

Dunk Island, off the coast of Mission Beach in North Queensland, is almost certainly the inspiration for the tropical island paradise in the novel. The island had become quite famous by the 1920s because of several popular books published since 1908 by "Beachcomber", a former journalist named Edmund Banfield who quit civilisation and moved to the uninhabited island with his wife in 1897. Between 1908 and 1925 he published a number of books in which he shared his observations on tropical nature, Aboriginal customs and reflections on his own life. Wenz would have read and admired his writings and used them as a basis for his own novel.

The other island whose presence looms in the final chapters of the novel is, of course, New Caledonia. Wenz, who had spent some time there himself in 1895, had a long fascination with the history of this French possession in the South Pacific, and he uses it several times in his writings. Perhaps he saw it as a kind of negative reflection of Australia, with its penal colony, and its patchy settlement by immigrants who turned to cattle raising and mining activities.

New Caledonia was annexed as a French colony in 1853. The French government established a penal colony there which was in operation from 1864 to 1924, and over the course of its operation approximately 21,000 prisoners from France were deported there. Its establishment provoked controversy and opposition in the Australian colonies, especially New South Wales and Queensland, which were still emerging from their own recent past as hosts of penitentiary establishments. There were three types of convicts: the most numerous were the common law criminals deported there for sentences ranging from eight years to life. They were mostly condemned to hard labour and were held in the penitentiary on

Nou Island, a small island forming part of the port of Noumea, the main city. At the end of their sentences, these prisoners would be released into the colony and were usually given a small land grant. They were not permitted to return to France. The second category were the "deportees", political prisoners who were mostly participants in the Paris Commune of 1871. They were usually held under less onerous conditions in the penitentiary on the Ile des Pins, and were granted an amnesty in 1880 which permitted them to return to France. The final category, numbering less than 4,000, were repeat offenders, who were sent to the colony from France after 1885. The practice of deporting convicts to New Caledonia ceased in 1897, but the penitentiary continued to operate for the convicts with long sentences, and other convicts who were already there had to spend the rest of their lives in the colony.

Historically, there were a small number of escapees from the first two categories who ended up in Australia. The exact number is unknown, but a few celebrity political deportees, such as Henri Rochefort and Louise Michel, became quite well known in Australia at the time. Our escapee in this novel, Louis Buffet, is a prisoner who had been sentenced to eight years' hard labour: this would presumably have been before 1897. If he arrived on the tropical island as an escapee in about 1910, he would already have completed his sentence but was condemned to stay in New Caledonia. Perhaps Wenz is applying a dose of poetic licence to blur the time scale a bit here: Louis could have been sentenced in 1897, in which case he would be serving that sentence until 1905, only a few years before our previous proposal for dating the novel.

Why would Wenz have chosen to blur the historical setting for his novel in this way? In fact, this historical blurring was already common practice in all his bush stories, right up to his final novel *L'Echarde* (1931). These stories are all set in an almost legendary past, a kind of 'dreamtime', covering the late colonial period from about 1870 to 1900. They compose a self-enclosed world that is already becoming a site of comforting nostalgia at the time of their first publication.

His second novel, *Le pays de leurs pères (Their Father's Land)* is both his most contemporary and most historically specific work. Composed in 1917-18, it is set in precisely the same time frame as the events it depicts. Part of its force comes from its documentary-like realism. His next novel, *Le Jardin des Coraux (A Coral Eden)*, was composed almost a decade later. Though it presents another documentary-like view of a recognisably modern Australia, Wenz deliberately avoids any mention or reference to the Great War. Given that the war had become almost an obsessive memory for Australians (and Europeans) of the 1920s, his choice to hark back to the more optimistic and prosperous period of early Federation Australia before the war for this novel might at first seem somewhat curious.

While emphasising the contemporary details of this novel's setting, I think Wenz is also making another kind of 'dreamtime' for the new nation. He chooses to remind us of the youthful and dynamic optimism of this period, even though he shows it being crushed by the resurgence of ghosts from the past (in the form of the convict escapee). But despite the tragedy of the novel's climax, the book ends on a more gentle note, evoking a hopeful future embodied by the young child of the novel's central couple. In this way, *A Coral Eden* can be seen as a glimpse into the future prospects of the new nation, even if there may be setbacks on the way, rather than a cosy remembrance of things past.

A
Coral
Eden

ONE

Australians claim that Sydney Harbour is the most beautiful harbour in the world. Travellers who have not seen the bay of Rio de Janeiro totally share this opinion. However that may be, Sydney Harbour is indisputably magnificent: it was even more admirable twenty years ago before its inlets and headlands were covered with a rash of red tiles and its hills capped with tall buildings in which humans are housed like guinea pigs.

The city itself is completely lacking in picturesque detail; its principal streets are all narrow and noisy with the din of the trams: only Macquarie Street, which has on it two hundred or so doctors and surgeons, possesses an aristocratic air, alongside George and Pitt Streets, which are at once middle and lower-middle class.

In the inner suburbs, there are fine dwellings lost amid splendid gardens; around the foreshores of the harbour one has visions of Italian lakes, glimpses of tropical isles, silhouettes of palm trees, banana trees and masses of greenery studded with red hibiscus.

An avenue lined with fig trees runs alongside Rose Bay whose blue waters rock a flotilla of yachts of all sizes. The other side of the avenue is bordered by gardens and flowered terraces in the middle of which stand quaint cottages with deep verandahs.

Talanga, the house of Doctor Kirving, was built right at the end of this avenue, on a promontory from which Sydney Harbour can be seen shimmering with light and life; no vessel could sail out of the port without passing before this property.

On the lawn of buffalo grass, green as a billiard table and soft as a deep pile carpet, Joan Kirving, seated in the shade of a tall mimosa, was playing with a very young dog to which she had given the name "Snowy". The small black spaniel, in no way affected by such an ill-suited designation, used all his energy in playing with his companion and nibbled her with all his bat-like teeth.

The animal's grunts accompanied the girl's giggles, and in a short moment of silence you could hear the rumbling of a large vehicle which came to a halt in front of the neighbouring house. Joan appeared very interested for a second, but then Snowy reminded her that the game was not over by trying to gobble one of her fingers. Their play resumed with more vigour.

A few minutes later, a ball of sky blue paper fell onto the lawn just within Joan's reach; another one followed, golden yellow in colour. The girl raised her eyes and saw above the hedge which marked the boundary of the neighbouring garden an unruly mop of hair of a fine auburn colour, bordering on reddish purple.

As a well brought up young girl, Joan pretended at first to have seen nothing and carried on teasing the dog. But as the multi-coloured projectiles began to accumulate on the grass around her, she raised her head.

The youth with the red-gold fleece spoke: "We're the new neighbours; I have come on ahead with the cupboards and wardrobes and Richard ... our cockatoo."

These explanations transformed the situation. There was nothing more to object to as far as good manners were concerned.

"Come and see my dog," said Joan to reduce as far as possible any appearance of curiosity. She was about to show the redhead how to get through the hedge; but the boy, familiar with such obstacles, was standing next to her in the blink of an eye. He patted the dog and took from his pocket some other balls of paper, saying as he offered them: "My father makes these ... our name is written on them, look: MacGillie."

He unfolded one of the papers and presented Joan with a caramel of the smoothest creaminess, one of those caramel toffees commonly called 'lock-jaws' by young children, who consume quite a lot of them.

"Jock MacGillie is my name."

"I am Joan Kirving: papa is a doctor."

The young lady was very tactful and she instantly regretted the last part of her sentence; the difference between the manufacturer of very chewy toffees and a doctor had something quite shocking about it, thought Joan; but Jock, without seeming to notice any such thing, offered a sweet to Snowy. The spaniel soon found himself in distress: it required the prompt intervention of the two youngsters to free him from this thing which stuck to his palate.

"I'll go and get Richard for you," said Jock. "He's a great bird: he only speaks Japanese, so you never know if he's being polite or not."

Joan noticed the agility with which Jock, coming back, got through the hedge while holding a large cage. The cockatoo noticed it as well, but aloud, and in Japanese.

The bird, with his eye round and black like a boot button, looked at the dog busy shredding an apple green ball of paper, opened out his sulphur crest like a fan, and expressed his quite personal opinion of the canine race, still in the foreign tongue.

"You'll have to teach him English," said Joan; "it's annoying never to know whether to laugh or be shocked."

The two youngsters carried on chatting like old acquaintances. Richard had dozed off; during the removal process he had gone through many emotions and made numerous efforts to maintain his dignity and his centre of gravity. The dog, worn out, had gone to sleep on the lawn, all crumpled up like a little black jumper.

Joan stood up and gave Jock a tour of the garden. Palm trees nodded their heads gently, banana trees allowed the breeze to play with their tattered leaves, and everywhere fat rose bushes presented their solid masses, extravagant with their colour and perfume. The lawn stretched right down to the water and up to a rocky outcrop which had been hollowed out to form a swimming pool. In the middle of the lawn rose a strange massive pillar made of corals of all shapes — small shrubs, sponges, bushes — whose deathly whiteness shone out in the sunlight.

"Captain Ross brought all that back from Queensland," said Joan; "he sailed his steam yacht along the Great Barrier Reef, and he said it is one of the most beautiful things he has ever seen."

Jock had stopped to admire a large font big enough to bathe a child in.

"That clam shell killed a native woman," added Joan, "The two valves closed on both her hands, and the woman was drowned in four feet of water."

They inspected the swimming pool: Joan confessed that she didn't like to swim in it any more since an octopus had got in and devoured a crayfish caught in the net.

The two of them sat on the rock and looked out over the blue water of the bay. The ferries sailed back and forth laden with picnickers who were going to Manly, to Watsons Bay, to anywhere it was possible to spend a few hours without hearing the clanking noise of the trams.

Joan pointed out to him, a few hundred yards offshore, the small boat belonging to Jack London, the *Snark*, which had been moored there since its return voyage from the Solomon Islands.

They discovered that they shared a love for the sea.

It was not the infinite extent of the Ocean which seduced them, but its varied shores, its desert islands which to them seemed to be still inhabited by ghosts, pirates and adventurers. Joan informed her new friend that she only ever read books written for boys, and that of all the sports she preferred swimming. Jock blushed with pleasure as much as his freckles would allow him to, and revealed at the same time that he had not been a brilliant student at school but that he had always won the swimming prizes.

The maid came to tell them that tea was served, and Joan, who knew the customs of Australian hospitality, simply asked Jock to follow her.

Without any false shyness, he accepted muffins and other cakes, and enjoyed them with the conviction of his age. Joan noticed that the boy was not used to the small tea napkins; he left his spoon in his cup and preferred to eat the cakes without the aid of a fork. In the course of their conversation, they discovered that they had both lost their mother, and this coincidence gave them a strange feeling of bonding.

After tea, the mistress of the house showed her guest the smoking room, the most curious room in *Talanga*, a small museum of objects from the Pacific. Joan gave Jock a thrill of pleasure when she showed him the arrows from Santa Cruz poisoned simply with the mud from the marshes where the mangroves grow and where thousands of one-armed crabs swarm. She showed him a skull from New Guinea with eyes of pearl-shell and a nose of red ochre, a caricature of the Grim Reaper which shows how much death is familiar and life is cheap in those fortunate islands. Below a long javelin, of which the pointed tip was made from a human tibia, a palm leaf hat hung on a nail.

"The executioner at Nou Island sold it to papa," said Joan, "allowing that the man to whom it had belonged had no more need of it since four o'clock that morning." Jock would have willingly examined other horrible things, but he didn't forget, amongst all these little excitements, the duties imposed on him by the removal. The men were still busy when Jock got back to his new home. The items of furniture, duly labelled, had been placed in the order that had been assigned to them. The removalists would have to come back the next day with the rest of the things: Jock sent them off, giving each of them a handful of toffees.

The young man, whose mind was essentially practical, set up his father's bedroom as best he could, made the two beds, set up the table in the dining room, and put the kettle on the gas in the kitchen.

He tried out the electricity in the various rooms to make sure that everything was working properly; then he took a tour of the property. The garden was neglected; the previous tenants had had little time to devote to horticulture: a few nice trees were growing there, but the bare, unhealthy looking lawn made a contrast with the grass covered paths scattered with wildflowers and sprouting shoots. In his fifteen-year-old mind Jock noted that they should take on a gardener urgently, otherwise he would not be able to invite his neighbour to visit this patch of land which looked more like a backyard than a garden. However, he liked the terrace of rocks which ran along the foreshore, and from which you could look out on a large part of the bay.

MacGillie senior, who had never taken on city ways, sounded a loud cooee as soon as he arrived at the house, and his paternal greetings went no further than a "Hello, Jock", to which Jock responded with a "Well, Dad" which was equally cordial and laconic. It was brief; but in these few words were concentrated all of the affection of two beings who loved each other deeply.

Father and son ate their meal cold at a table covered with pages of a newspaper. Old Mac drank his tea in small sips while listening to the details of the different stages of the removal process.

"Dad," said the boy as he fished out the last sardine which seemed to be wallowing in the disembowelled tin, "I have met the young girl next door; she is very nice, her father is a doctor."

Both men were busy washing up the crockery and the cutlery which they had used sparingly, like all those who must take on themselves this thankless task, when the front door knocker sounded. Doctor Kirving came in and introduced himself. "Good evening, neighbour, come over and have a pipe at my place, and make yourself welcome; my daughter and your son have met already."

MacGillie, who liked plain dealing, accepted the invitation and, followed by Jock, accompanied the doctor back to his house. Joan was introduced, after which she dragged off her new friend into the garden to show him the *Ortala* which was arriving from London, huge and majestic and lit up as for a nocturnal celebration.

"Later on, in a few years' time," said the young lady, "Papa wants to send me over to Europe; it must be lovely to travel on a grand boat like that one"

"I would like to travel too," said Jock; "I would love to see Scotland; Dad speaks of it so often, even though he left it when he was sixteen."

Meanwhile, the two older men got to know each other amid the smoke of their pipes; they had already found some things in common: both had been born in Scotland, both were widowed; both had worked at sea, and had arrived in Australia on sailing ships, at a time when the voyage was made in five months sailing via Saint Helena and the Cape.

Their distant memories arose one after another, revealing themselves suddenly, emerging unexpectedly, heterogeneous, multi-coloured, as if coming out of a magician's hat; they crossed the equator and verged on the poles like the feathery trails of marine currents on a globe of the world.

Then Mac, proud of his humble origins, recalled the Scottish Sundays which, in his youth, had been weekly nightmares; three divine services; readings, words and gestures appropriate to a gloomy Sabbath.

At the age of sixteen, Dave MacGillie had refused to believe that the Good Lord had created men for the sole purpose of boring them stupid: nevertheless, he had wanted to assure himself of this by seeking to live in another environment. There was only one step to take – he took it – from the dock at Dundee onto the deck of a vessel called *Pride of the North*.

The sea was rough, the food awful and the bunks narrow; but at least, on board, Sunday was no plainer than the other days.

"Sailor, miner, confectioner," said Mac animatedly, "there's a series of occupations where you can't quite see the connections; but you, a cabin boy on board the *Mary Anne*, and yet you became a doctor.

"Here am I, the most modest of men, I see the name MacGillie on every wall, in the trams, in the railway stations; on footpaths, on the back of postage stamps, and even on tooth-picks. That's what the trade demands. You can sell sawdust; you only have to colour it pink, flavour it with mint, pack it in small tins: advertise it as Egyptian Dental Powder and you've got every chance of making a fortune.

"My sweets are my most useful advertising agents: the smooth toffee sticks the sweet wrappers everywhere. Do you realise that I produce fifty-eight different varieties? Every one of them has its name. The conversation candies are very successful: one sugar heart says 'Do you love me?', another one replies 'That depends'. It's too stupid for words; but young people love it, and I really think a quarter pound of these candies has more than once been enough to lead to an engagement. We manufacture licorice shoelaces, mice and frogs; nineteen different sorts of chocolates, nougats, marzipans, jujubes and barley sugars.

"That makes you laugh, doctor; it amuses me as well. But everything I sell is good, and my merchandise always makes people happy."

The doctor really was laughing, for MacGillie looked more like an old topsailman than a confectioner.

Kirving, for his part, looked like a smiling Savonarola full of humour. He had retained from his sailing days some expressions which had many a time startled his lady patients: but the confidence inspired by his wide open eyes cancelled out his blunt speech, and this gaze used to scanning the horizon seemed to see straight into people's state of mind as well as the ills from which they were suffering.

"Well," said the doctor, "I have always admired the self-made man, the one who has honestly hauled himself up by the strength of his hands. The man born into money is much less appealing to me; he always reminds me of a ready-made suit. The patients who interest me the most are those who can barely afford to pay me: my best friend,

Captain Ross, is as poor as Job; but he is a remarkable man with a very fine character. I will introduce him to you one day."

Captain Ross and Doctor Kirving had met, years before, somewhere in the Pacific. Their love of the sea had brought them together; the strong personality of the skipper had made from the beginning a positive impact on the doctor, which was the origin of a solid friendship.

After intervals of months, or even years, the wind would bring Ross to *Talanga* where he was always welcomed with open arms. He was well loved, and he always had some new story to tell. The only thing the captain boasted about openly and unashamedly was that he numbered among his ancestors a companion of Drake and Hawkins who had fought against the Invincible Armada. It was no doubt because of this tradition piously maintained in his family that he sported a goatee and a handle-bar moustache which, with his hooked nose and short haircut, gave him the look of a gentleman pirate from the time of Queen Bess.

Moreover, he had always been a bit of a buccaneer and for the last fifteen years had criss-crossed the South Seas trying his hand at everything. One day when he returned from a six-month cruise to the Caroline Islands, a love affair which ended badly had caused him to return the next day to his vessel. Once he got to Tahiti he lived the life of a savage for more than a year, far from the company of men of his own colour; the betrayal by a woman seemed to have permanently turned him against his whole race.

This voluntary exile finally had a calming effect and had freed him of all the bitterness which had occupied his heart. He had reboarded his ketch, and the breeze blowing over the water had dissipated the last clouds of his bad memories. He felt himself a new man, with a whole new outlook on life; he underwent a rebirth which affected all the muscles of his young body tanned and salted by the sun and the sea.

He had discovered that life is not just one story, that it is made up of chapters which you can try to forget in order to commence new ones. Bravely, with no ill feelings, he had begun again. He had dived for pearls in the Marquesas with only modest success, then around

Thursday Island in the Torres Strait, and even as far as the Arru Islands near Dutch New Guinea.

Two good seasons had put him back on his feet; and since he always sought adventure rather than money, he drifted idly from the Marianas to Samoa, calling in at palm-fringed atolls. His transactions in the various islands were generally satisfactory; but unfortunately he brought back from the Bismarck Archipelago a barbed spear point lodged in his shoulder.

After two hours of waiting, Ross dared hope that the weapon was not poisoned and that tetanus would not break out; he set sail for the nearest port, where he found an amateur surgeon who was able to extract from him eight fish bones fixed with diabolical skill to a spear point carved from a human tibia.

With his shoulder in pain, Ross set out for Sydney where he took a well earned rest. It was then that he resumed his contacts with Doctor Kirving. Young Joan never wearied of hearing about his adventures and was overjoyed when she received the gift of the corals and sea shells that Ross had brought back from his voyages.

He had talked about the Great Barrier Reef that parallels the Queensland coast for 1,250 miles; it is made up of living corals of many colours, madrepores, huge shells, and fish of various shapes whose colours are as vivid and brilliant as those of tropical birds.

Joan followed the traces of the captain's large finger over the map, and from that moment on the idea got firmly fixed in her head that one day she would go off to see all these marvels. It was a dream which she took pleasure in cultivating – a dream that she was sure she would realise some day.

A few days after getting to know Jock she had spoken to him of her plans, and he, enthusiastic, had offered to go with the girl on this expedition.

This 'Coral Eden' – as Captain Ross had called it - became from then on an obsession for the two youngsters. While waiting out the indefinite time until they could undertake this voyage, they spent their leisure time in the dinghy tied up at Doctor Kirving's jetty.

A rocky outcrop jutted out of the water a hundred yards off the shore of the garden; a solitary tree had grown on it. The harbour picnickers did not venture into this area, for the islet was surrounded by reefs at water level: Joan knew the only channel which allowed access to what she called her island. It may not have been a large island, but it was a private world surrounded by deep blue water.

Its tiny beach where they moored the dinghy, the gaps in the rock against which the rising tide lapped with loud kissing sounds, were places of mystery in the eyes of the two youngsters; and beneath the solitary tree the young pirates often set up a tent and lit a fire with some wood brought from the garden. Fingers were burnt on the billy full of tea, and great feasts of cakes were had. They fished, and sometimes even caught something; they chattered as they watched the yachts fly by like white birds frightened by a hawk.

"I have always dreamed of having my own island," said Joan; "I think that almost everybody would like to have one. We are too crowded together on land, people make too much noise, talk too much."

Jock, who had spent most of his childhood on a deserted plain in a natural environment quite different from the one that was now around him, had accepted the idea of an island as something completely indispensable in life.

Dressed in their bathing costumes, the two kids warmed themselves for hours in the sun, and took turns going in the water, for you had to have someone keeping an eye out for sharks. These awful creatures were not often found in this part of the harbour, but you never knew: they had been sometimes seen out in Rose Bay and at Watsons Bay.

The books that they read were, of course, Robinson Crusoe-like stories and tales of pirates; they regretted living in an age when most of the freebooters carried out their exploits on solid ground, with no great risks or dangers.

TWO

This new friendship had put Joan into a more contemplative state of mind; the young man had pleased her with his frankness and by that atmosphere of the bush which seemed to emanate from him. He smelled of eucalyptus, open air, dust and even the sun from the outback: his many freckles made you think of an over-exposed photographic print.

MacGillie said it himself: 'Jock was a rough diamond', adding that something could be made of him with patience and emery. The young boy had been brought up on the goldfields, in a region where the sun was a constant obsession and water was as precious as the coveted metal. You couldn't dream of taking a daily bath in a liquid that came from far away in water carts or by camel. Jock, and others around him, put up with this privation philosophically.

Stoic Mother MacGillie did not have a great house to look after; the size of their hut was about that of a dining room carpet, but she had just as much to occupy herself with, for the boy alone provided enough reasons to keep her busy.

MacGillie worked at first on the claim which belonged to him; but he was digging himself slowly and without conviction down to the centre of the earth, and after a few months of pointless effort he had put his pick and shovel at the service of a neighbour who still had a few grand illusions and a certain imagination which Mac no longer had. For a year he worked for other men and was thus able to put a little money aside.

One Saturday afternoon, when each man had carefully performed his ablutions with the contents of a single bucket of water per person, MacGillie and his family were strolling down the main street of the struggling little town. They stopped in front of the general store where they sold tools, corsets, tinned jam and dynamite. A jar of English sweets displayed in the window attracted Jock's attention, while his father was admiring a pair of boots which were definitely meant for a well-off miner. The child had been asking for sweets for a long time. Mac went into the store determined to win possession of the jar.

"Five shillings and sixpence," said the shopkeeper unceremoniously. Mac took the blow without flinching and paid up with the air of a blasé millionaire.

Scotsmen take to certain specific professions. Four-fifths of the world's ships have mechanics who were born not far from Glasgow; the best judges of cattle or sheep are often of the same origin (the Irishman looks after horses and pigs). Old Caledonia also supplies stonemasons whose funerary monuments are well designed to reconcile the living with existence.

Finally, the Scots seem to have a special aptitude for confectionery: having planted sugar cane for a long time in the colonies, they have no doubt discovered that you can make more money melting sugar than growing it. That same evening, while Jock was finishing enjoying his sweets in the company of some mates, Mac and his wife were secretly trying out some experiments which produced smells of burning sugar. A large metal drum, which had once contained tar, was transformed into a boiler, and in the week which followed, the MacGillie sweet factory had already built up a faithful clientele among the local ill-shod youth.

The ex-miner had no intention of remaining an amateur; a month later he had in his hands a volume of three hundred pages which dealt with the art of the confectioner, from the boiling of vulgar barley sugar to the preparation of Montélimar nougats. This sickly study carried out in one go opened up for Mac a new window into the future; the support of his wife allowed him to abandon the uncertain process which consists in transforming human sweat and patience into fine gold.

A new shop opened up in the main street of Western Star: it sold fruits which had grown four hundred miles away, newspapers that were several weeks old, books, and 'home made' toffees. Mac soon dreamed of quitting the bush for the city: he took a job in Perth in a sweet factory, worked as an apprentice, learned all that he could, while his wife kept a small shop which allowed Jock to get some education.

The city did not impress the little savage who blew in from the Western Desert; he had reached that age of ten years at which the critical instinct is more developed than the power of admiration. When he saw the sea for the first time, one Sunday when his parents had taken him to Fremantle, he looked at it for a while without saying a word, went up to a wave dying away on the sand, plunged his fingers into it and said:

"It's true, it really is salty... well then, all that water is no good for anything"

This disenchanted observation did not prevent him from gazing out at the expanse of blue: for a long while he stood there motionless, speechless before this silky sparkling immensity.

He did not understand either why people settled down on top of each other in cities like sheep herded into a yard by barking dogs. School was a new experience for him; he became popular in his first week, on the very day he came home as the proud owner of an eye developing the appearance of a rainbow in a tropical sunset. His mother pointed out that the Bible did not approve of revenge: Jock respectfully reminded her that another passage from the Bible recommended charity; the boy who had given him this black eye had received in return a pair of the same colour.

The 'rough diamond' made his way in this new environment; Jock had a lively intelligence, practical and utilitarian: he was already aware that intelligence could be transformed into pounds sterling. He showed a strange facility to adapt, an unquenchable thirst for knowledge and an interesting urge to develop both his body and his mind; in that, he was following the example of his father who, with bumpy progress and by the strength of his own hands, was hoisting himself higher every day. Indeed, Old Mac was not wasting any time; he was learning everything he could lay his hands on, and in the evenings he would often drag Jock off to a public library, where they would each fossick among the books like miners trying to strike it lucky.

Some time later, Mac had received a business offer: the firm of Gow and MacGillie was launched and took off like a balloon; then the fellow quitted the West for Sydney, the sprawling city which sucked in the population from the countryside and crowded it into the new suburbs that it spewed out like flows of lava.

Each city has its own atmosphere: Peking has one that is unique, indescribable; London's is a mixture of fish and hops; that of Paris alternates between the scent of Houbigant and the odour of drains. Sydney has the smell of fried foods and the stale exhalations of its many sweet factories which sell their merchandise wholesale or in large pallet loads. It is a greedy town, something Mac realised straight away, and when his associate Gow sold him his share in order to return to his beloved Scotland, Sydney quickly learned to spell his name on cartons and wrappers of every colour.

Everything seemed to favour the former miner; he fully enjoyed that supreme satisfaction of having accomplished something; he had made it to the top of the heap after a long climb. It was then that his best mate Janet died. Mac, stunned by such a blow, at first refused to accept what had been dealt to him by a fate that was blind and deaf.

Joan Kirving, at fourteen, was not a great beauty; but she was more promising, she had all that was needed to become an attractive person. Under the big Australian sun she had grown like bamboo; her bearing and her gestures still had the charming and amusing awkwardness that can be found in the children of humans, just as in the young of animals. Her features were still developing; her wide-set blue eyes, almost blue-grey, lit up an oval face framed by two heavy plaits of chestnut brown hair that she let fall onto her shoulders.

Joan and Jock soon felt that they could have no more secrets from each other; that was what their friendship required. Sitting on the edge of the terrace overlooking the harbour, their legs hanging over the gently lapping water, they exchanged their thoughts and made their confessions to each other.

Joan would have liked to be a man, to roam the world, have adventures, stride through sands and dead leaves that no other human foot had ever touched. She would sail often to those deserted beaches that Ross had talked about, to the coasts where grew those corals that she had loved all through her childhood in this garden. They held within their cells the strange smell of mysterious, faraway seas; and in the darkness of night they shed their phosphorescent whiteness on the lawn. The giant conch shells had since long ago sounded out the ceaseless roaring of the shores where serried ranks of coconut trees were lined up, tossing their heads in the sea breeze.

"Jock, I want to go where men have not yet ventured. Just think, a cove of untouched sand, a little creek with no tin cans or lemonade bottles, no newspapers or waste paper blown about by the wind; how beautiful that must be! A beach with no broken glass, no corks, no old shoes"

"Yes," Jock mused aloud, "that must be beautiful; but you'd

have to go a long way from Sydney to find that."

Joan, her eyes sparkling, threw one plait over her shoulder just as she did whenever an idea excited her, and continued: "When I get back from Europe, I want to go up there and visit these beaches white as snow, as the snow that I have never seen. Jock, we shall go together."

And Jock, in all sincerity, promised Joan once again that he would go with her to see her Coral Eden.

Often, on a Saturday afternoon, Doctor Kirving would take them out on his small yacht; MacGillie would accompany them and the team of four would work as one man. The youngsters were becoming expert in the handling of the sails as well as with the rudder. In one of the numerous coves, they would seek out a spot that the picnickers had not yet invaded, and while the billy was on the fire Joan and Jock would get into the water just next to the boat.

Mac and the doctor got along perfectly; the diversity of their everyday lives allowed them to talk shop without boring each other.

"She's a fine slip of a girl," said Mac to the doctor as he watched Joan getting out of the water.

"Jock is a well built young man," added Kirving, as someone who knew what he was talking about; "They both swim like porpoises, it's a pleasure to watch them."

He always felt relaxed on these weekends; he had left his medical seriousness behind in his consulting rooms on Macquarie Street. His patients would not have recognised him, wearing his old sailor's cap and dressed like a fisherman from Manly.

"Huh! Mac, you must be glad to sniff a bit of salt; it's a change from the saccharine atmosphere of your toffees. For me, it's a real moment of escape during which I can forget about this bunch of cracked, broken or irreparable things which is humanity. Just think, forty-eight hours without hearing those sordid confessions of sick people, without having to reassure the lunatics, cheer up the moribund, lie to the incurables!

"Given we live in an era of egalitarian lack of respect, one sometimes feels like making a few observations to the Good Lord about the standard of his work. Could he not, for example, have made man like a Black Forest cuckoo clock, with a minimum of uncomplicated cogs enclosed in a solid wooden box? Instead of that, he has constructed precision chronometers set with rubies; but a speck of dust is enough to clog up the mainspring, and for us, the clockmakers, it is not very often that we are able to repair them."

"Personally," added Mac, "I think that the Creator, when he first constructed man, had no idea of the possibilities ... and the impossibilities of the strangest of all creatures. He is certainly a very intelligent being sometimes; but as you say, he is terribly fragile and his own powers are very limited; he doesn't swim well and he can't fly. It has taken him centuries and all his genius to finally manage to imitate the duck."

"You know," said the doctor gesturing to Joan and Jock who were drying themselves in the sun and keeping an eye on the billy that they had removed from the fire, "over there are two young people who don't worry themselves too much about humanity; let's go and see if we can have some lunch."

"Jock," said the young lady lying on the beach beside her friend, "what is there that is more blue than the sea, warmer than the sun, softer than the sand?"

The boy shook his head as if he had no answer to give; but it suddenly came to him that there was something more blue, more warm and more soft than all this.

One day in summer Joan suggested to Jock that they go for a swim at Coogee; they took the tram, each carrying under their arm their swimming costume rolled up in a towel. Despite the early morning hour the heat was already heavy; their compartment was full of passengers laden with baskets full of provisions, or carrying those small pieces of luggage known as 'attaché cases' which were more often used for carrying bottles than diplomatic documents. Children were in the majority, nibbling biscuits or taking bites of bananas. They were mostly blond: even the Australian sun cannot manage to change the Anglo-Saxon physical type.

On arriving at the terminus at Coogee, the two friends were not surprised to see that the beach was densely swarming with people; the ocean seemed to be fringed with a foam of humanity: people were bathing shoulder to shoulder.

Coogee is a highly popular beach; it is not a big beach, but Sydney disgorges there tramloads of its population eager for fresh air, sun and salt water. In the middle of the crescent of white sand formed by the bay rises a metal tower topped by a platform on which two men ceaselessly scan the sea with binoculars, and have a large bell within reach.

On the beaches of Australia a painter would have no trouble finding some good models among the bathers. Their swimming has developed them magnificently and the sun has artfully coloured them golden brown.

Joan and Jock each went in their own direction to get undressed in their cabin; they soon rejoined each other at the foot of the tower where they had arranged to meet. She had the figure of a young nymph; one of the shoulder straps of her black costume had slipped down, revealing on her tanned skin a thin white line where the sun had not reached. Jock, too, was well built; but all the skin that his trunks revealed seemed to have been sprayed by a hail of freckles which had not missed a square inch of him.

The two of them tacked between the groups of people stretched out on the sand, working their way through this crowd which seemed to have abandoned their bourgeois character along with their clothes and which had been refined and rendered more attractive by their semi-nudity. They went into the water, forced their way through the thick fringe of bathers and eventually found themselves in an area where they could swim at their ease and plunge into the crystal blue waves which followed uninterruptedly one after the other.

Soon far removed from the bathers, they frolicked like dolphins, swimming in each other's wake, in the manner of Pacific islanders whose technique has been taken up all over the world. Suddenly a sound bounced off the water and ricocheted into their ears: they both understood immediately, and said at the same time: "Sharks!" They turned back, and letting themselves ride on the crest of several large breakers, they caught sight of the lookouts who were waving at them. Loads of bathers were rushing back to the beach, while the bell kept tolling.

They saw the surfboat coming towards them, rowed by a team of solid lads in their bathers. Jock called out to Joan to swim with all her might towards the boat; instead of hurrying himself, he slowed down and let his companion go first. He looked over his shoulder and saw what he dreaded to see: the great blade of the dorsal fin was slicing through the water fifty yards away from him. Then he saw that Joan was almost in reach of the lifeboat; he did a few strokes of dog-paddling so as to make as much noise as possible. It was only when he saw Joan was on the boat and waving at him that he put all his strength into it.

The front of the lifeboat raised up by the waves looked to him like the threatening prow of a ship; at the same time, it only seemed to be making slowly towards him and he felt he was only gaining on it by inches.

While he was struggling with all his willpower, with all the angry strength of his body, his eyes blinded by the salt water, he suddenly realised that he was in a race against death. While the seconds sped past — or rather the centuries! — he thought he was going to lose the struggle; then he felt a furious impatience because the inevitable was approaching so slowly. At that moment a thought came to him and wrapped its great wings around him, soft and caressing: Joan was safe. The horrible thing behind him no longer seemed so terrifying: Joan was safe. For a fraction of a second, while he felt his whole being shattered, his arms ripped out of his shoulders, and his legs weighed down with fatigue, he thought he could hear a voice calling him from the depths of the buzzing noise which hummed in his ears; he spat out some salt water and called out "Joan". He suddenly found himself up against a big white wall, he felt himself being hauled up, while oars struck out at the grey monster brushing against the bow of the boat.

Jock, now lying in the bottom of the boat, did not say a word, so much was he basking in the sudden soothing passivity and at the same time dreading to come out of a dream. Joan squeezed his arm, saying: "Jock dear." He smiled at his companion as he had never smiled before, and kissed her bare foot.

The oarsmen left their seats one after another: they all wanted to see the heroic lad who had simply and willingly made himself the bait for a shark, for a 'grey nurse' that was twelve feet long.

When Jock had got his breath back and felt all this attention weighing down on him, he said: "Thank you all ... it was a near thing ... that rotten cramp that seized me ..."

"Cramp, my eye" said one of the oarsmen who, in his near nakedness looked as handsome as a demi-god, but who was one of the great larrikins of Woolloomooloo.

Joan seemed not to notice the crude expression of this member of the crew; she kept looking at Jock. Muscled arms pulled on the long oars; vigorous legs braced themselves against the hull, and the men, hair flying, made the surfboat skim over the blue waves, as proud as Vikings bringing back a rich booty.

The beach, where an anxious crowd was gathering, applauded the life savers; but the latter raised their arms to wave this away. The demi-god from Woolloomooloo, standing on one of the small boats that the crowd had dragged up on the sand, said: "Keep all that for the kid" and when he had recounted everything they had seen in the surfboat, a circle formed around the little mermaid and her gallant knight and carried them away in triumph.

Several photographers were clamouring for the heroes; Joan and Jock, prisoners of their admirers, were set up for the 'pose'. Jock whispered a few words into his friend's ear; the plates and the films would register a frowning and unrecognisable couple. One reporter from the *Morning Sun* took out his notebook and asked for names and addresses, which were supplied by Jock who showed a remarkable disdain for the Sydney street directory.

"Her name is Fanny Trowell, and I am her brother Ernie; we live at number 7, Seaview Terrace, Redfern."

A discreet nudge to Joan was the signal to depart; they both had to shake all the hands as the Prince of Wales does on one of his tours; finally they managed to escape. A few minutes later, dressed, they found themselves at the tram terminus. The trip home was silent; both were worn out and their eyes were starting to close in spite of themselves. The two friends were considering just how necessary it was to find out their fathers' attitudes about sea bathing, considered as a sport. By mutual agreement, they decided that they would maintain silence about this adventure-packed morning.

The following day, Jock went to the newsagent who also sold MacGillie brand confectionery and bought a copy of the *Morning Sun*. The last page was covered with a great variety of photos: race horses, a football match and – for the eighth time in three weeks – the prettiest girl in Sydney. In a special box frame, made up of vegetation which unmistakably resembled laurel leaves, 'the Heroes of Coogee', Ernie Trowell and his sister, were scowling in the harsh light of the sun. They could relax about the resemblance, none of their friends would be able to recognise them.

The article, which Jock read as he zigzagged along the footpath, caused him several times to express aloud his opinion of journalists whose imagination surpasses that of other mortals. "Coogee Beach was yesterday the scene of a gripping drama witnessed by several thousand people. The shark alarm rang out, and the bathers, even though they were used to such alarms, suddenly seemed to be taking part in a desperate swimming race; to all appearances, the goal was the beach itself. Left alone, two bathers who had ventured further out swam at full speed towards the surfboat that was going to their rescue. The lifesavers first took on board a young girl; the young man who was with her had stayed behind to cover the escape of his friend. This act of heroism filled the crew with admiration; the swimmer, who was beginning to tire, nevertheless won by a nose his race against a fifteen-foot-long 'grey nurse'. The crew had to beat off the shark with their oars. As soon as they made it to the beach, the young hero and his companion were greeted by warm applause."

Jock remembered that the lifesavers had estimated the shark's length to be twelve feet; but reporters in all countries are always generous.

The hero folded up the newspaper to the smallest possible size and jammed it into his deepest pocket, vowing not to speak to Joan about the previous day's events. But immediately after breakfast, she called out to her neighbour over the garden hedge and asked: "Did you get the Morning Sun?"

Jock, like most lads of his age, could not tell a lie when you looked him in the eye. He fished out the newspaper from his pocket and passed it to Joan; she went over to the terrace and, her legs dangling over the water, she began to read it.

That same evening, while Doctor Kirving and MacGillie were playing their card game in the smoking room as stuffy as a tunnel, Joan gave Jock a glance which signified "Follow me." The boy obeyed, as if he had been expecting for some time the moment of explanation.

"Jock, I am going to ask you a question, just the one; you will only have to answer with one word, but choose it well." There followed a silence; deep down, Jock compared it to the pause between two hammer blows.

Joan went on: "Yesterday, when you were swimming, did you get a cramp, yes or no?"

With the back of his hand, Jock wiped his nose which had nothing aquiline about it and replied: "No."

"Well then, it's just as they said in the paper ... you stayed behind ... on purpose." Joan's large blue eyes were now glittering.

"Jock, darling, you risked everything for me ... I, Joan, am now yours for ever ... do you understand?"

That is how Jack Andrew MacGillie, aged sixteen years and three months, and Joan Mary Kirving, aged fifteen and a half years, became secretly engaged, with the moon as their only witness.

When they walked back across the lawn towards the house, that same moon lit up with a strange glow the corals of all kinds, the huge clam shells half open like dragons' jaws; and their glowing light, phosphorescent, shone with a whiteness which seemed to reflect the light of the beyond.

THREE

The years passed. Finally the day came when Joan had to buy herself some trunks and many things to fill them. Her father booked her a cabin on one of the Austral Company boats, and entrusted her care to some friends who were also to make the voyage. In London a young and lively aunt whom she only knew through her letters was to serve as both her hostess and her chaperone.

Joan made her preparations without much pleasure; her friends, envious of her good fortune, could not understand how she could keep so calm amid the gaping trunks, the opened boxes and a rising tide of tissue paper.

On the eve of her departure, the MacGillies were invited to dinner: everyone made an effort to give the meal an appearance of cheerfulness. When the pipes were lit, Old Mac told how, during one of his voyages, he had experienced two Good Fridays in forty-eight hours at sea off the Fiji Islands when he was making sail for Vancouver. The doctor recalled a mutiny in the harbour of Talcahuano: his cutter the *Saucy Sally* was taking on barrels of a Chilean wine heading for Europe ... to be naturalised in Bordeaux.

Joan took Jock out onto the little terrace. They walked across the garden in silence. They walked arm in arm, and this contact seemed to have joined them one to the other in body and soul; their mixed up thoughts were carried away by the same current. Their thoughts were so similar that neither one considered uttering them aloud. For the first time in their young life they felt the torments of separation rising towards their heart like an ice-cold tide, like a death slow in coming. They sat down on the edge of the terrace, in their favourite position, with their legs dangling over the water, as if the sea was the friend they chose to have near them, the sole witness of their farewells. Without saying anything, they watched the lights of the ferries gliding over the water: the red and green beacons, the lights on deck giving the air of some nautical festival to the harbour as busy as a boulevard. One boat was coming back from Watsons Bay, laden with day-trippers: a band was playing, throwing out as it passed by some snatches of a waltz which seemed to float like down on the surface of the water; and these skimming notes came to them, sad, in the gentle night.

Joan spoke first. "Eighteen months, Jock! Eighteen long months over there. When we see each other again, you will be twenty-two, and I will be twenty-one ... I am afraid of these good-byes; I have been thinking about them for months. I see them like an iron curtain which descends slowly and is about to cut my existence in two. I don't remember ever having said any real farewells to Dad. Cheerio, yes; but not farewell. I have felt all the horror of separation ... that time when you won that race against ... the 'grey nurse'; I thought I would never see you again, I closed my eyes for seconds, terrified I would hear the panicked cries of the men who had lost hope of saving you.

"Farewell, it is a word in which there is as much fear as hope; we feel so fragile, we are so afraid of the distance which tears us apart from the ones we love; absence seems to us the sister of death. Even men who believe in nothing say 'Adieu' without realising that they are asking a divinity to watch over them.

"Dad, I know, is suffering too, he will suffer from knowing that I am far away from him; but he wants me to get to know the 'old country', to see the village where he was born and where his parents lived. That is a pilgrimage that all Australians undertake who can do so; the squatter from Thargomindah leaves his Queensland desert to go and visit his distant cousin who owns a house-boat on the Thames and some moors in Scotland.

"Tomorrow night I will be at sea, and every turn of the screw whose echo I hear through my pillow will put more ocean between us, Jock, my darling ..."

But Jock knew what she meant. "I will not forget you, not for a moment; I will keep an eye on your Dad as I would watch out for my own. When we see each other again, my mate, will you have changed much? Will you still be the same Joan, or will you have turned into Miss Kirving?"

"No," continued the young woman, "I will be what I am now. I know, you want to hear Joan tell you once more that she has promised herself to you ... Yes, Jock, I will come back, you only have to beckon me, Joan will be your wife."

Jock pulled her to him; without a word, without moving, they stood clinging together for a long time in darkness and silence.

They said their adieu in the dark, as if they were afraid of showing their too shiny eyes. They embraced for a long while and departed from each other like lovers, as if their separation had suddenly just forged a chain which linked them tightly to one another. They were lovers who had not yet known love … and they dreamed of it like a distant, unknown country; it was still only an amorous friendship which surrounded and caressed them, brushing their senses with its light wing.

"Good-bye, Joan, God bless you."

"Good-bye, Jock, God bless you."

And that was all. A shooting star slashed the sky with a long streak of fire and disappeared into a distance that the mind of man would never know.

On the quayside, the vendors had long sold out of their coloured streamers. The friends, all packed together into a solid mass, had thrown them towards the passengers leaning over the upper deck. These hundreds of streamers formed a many-coloured cascade linking the vessel to the shore, and these fragile ribbons held by hands that could no longer hold each other seemed to be the only moorings for the *Arvila*. Long was the wait that dreaded the final moment of departure; men, still holding streamers, their heads raised, were calling out scraps of conversation to the passengers; they were laughing, perhaps still under the influence of the farewell whiskies; women were weeping, and those brightly coloured streamers gave the whole scene a sad carnival air. The twenty thousand-ton monster, dominating the quayside with its five decks, was in reality no more shackled than an elephant: its huge funnels were steaming slowly and the gaping red maws of its ventilators were awaiting the moment when they would gulp down the air of the open sea.

Suddenly a plume of white steam gushed out: the *Arvila* roared the first of its farewells. Horn blasts gave the signal to go ashore to those who were not passengers. Twice more, the siren split the air: freed of its moorings, the monster was impatient to depart.

Very gradually, its great bulk moved away from the quay, three inches, six inches, and soon the water with its shimmering oil-slick and scattered with garbage was visible to the passengers leaning over and still holding the ends of their streamers. At that moment the streamers stiffened, snapped, and fluttered freely along the side of the *Arvila*. The crowd on the quayside gradually disappeared, their handkerchiefs the only visible detail, tossing about like seagulls in a storm.

For a long while Joan watched her father waving at her, but then distance and tears would only let her make out groups of people breaking up slowly and regretfully.

On the terrace of her garden, Jock had raised the signal for 'Bon voyage' up on the little flagpole which, every Sunday and holiday, flew the blue flag with the stars of the Southern Cross.

He recognised her with the aid of his binoculars while the vessel was sailing majestically past a few hundred yards away; she was alone, on the upper deck, waving her handkerchief. Jock waved back until the ship disappeared behind one of the headlands in the harbour. Then he crumpled in a heap on the terrace, and remained for an hour stretched out on his belly, his face pressed into his folded arms.

On the following days each morning was for him like the recommencement of a bad dream; a great emptiness had taken over his life, his days at college could not make him forget it, and coming home each evening made it all the more real. He wandered about in the garden at *Talanga*, revisiting every nook and cranny; the corals were still as white as ever, the giant clams still gaping wide; there was the terrace where they had talked about so many things together, the blue water that they had so often crossed over to get to their little island. Joan's presence filled the garden, she was everywhere; a tall Mexican cereus cactus still held a mauve silken thread which had belonged to one of her dresses. Sometimes Jock thought he heard her footsteps on the sandy garden path; he thought he could smell the dried flower perfume of her hair.

Doctor Kirving, too, often wandered about the garden; they would talk about the absent girl like father and son, they were both suffering from the same sadness.

Old MacGillie was not so demonstrative, but even he felt a certain pity; he saw his boy's distress and tried to cheer him up. Jock felt that a new faith had been born in him, a religion for him alone, created for her alone; a mute adoration of the absent one filled all of his thoughts, inspiring prayers and vows which arose from the depths of his soul. However life continued on as usual around him, and Jock had to admit that, even without her, the world continued on its way.

Joan, who was not affected by sea-sickness, found all sorts of distractions in the shipboard routine: she would walk the length of the deck, carefully measuring out the six circuits of the promenade deck which would allow her to cover the distance of a mile.

She noticed how quickly the very many children on the boat had adapted to their new environment; from their very first day they had discovered all of the ship's resources, with its hiding places and its ventilators.

Mr and Mrs James, to whom Doctor Kirving had entrusted his daughter, were fairly easy-going chaperones; they were only seen at mealtimes, for they spent their days and part of their nights around a bridge table.

In any case, Joan didn't need much monitoring; raised without many restrictions and used to going about the city as she pleased, she had acquired an instinct which allowed her to judge fairly exactly the people who were around her.

Sharing the James's table was a fat American who possessed a solid gold smile and talked exclusively of dollars and millions. Otherwise he was of excellent character. As early as the second meal, he confided in his fellow diners that he was the director of a firm that traded in sponges, "the biggest one in the world". He was returning from an exploratory trip along the coasts of Australia, and confessed that the sponges he had seen there were not worth much.

At the other end of the table sat a timid fellow, short and thin, who was coming back from New Guinea, where he had endured eight months of fever, amongst mosquitoes, crocodiles and savages who were cannibals, more or less. He was collecting butterflies and coleoptera for an important museum in Europe.

Joan naturally attracted a swarm of young men around her, she danced as much as she wanted; but she managed to escape the epidemic of engagements which broke out on board between Colombo and Cape Guardafui.

London disappointed her at first; she was expecting to see the city under its veil of fog, but this October day was sunny and basking in an autumn beauty brightened up by the golden yellow trees. She found it difficult to bear the sad sight of so many people standing on the city pavements trying to sell matches or ridiculous toys, painfully absurd in the hands of these starving and poorly dressed wretches. A great sadness overcame her; the spectacle of poverty was something new to her, and for the first time she was seeing it appear before her eyes.

This destitute crowd sought out the wealthy districts, their poverty was on display not far from the gentlemen's clubs of Piccadilly, in the parks or on Regent Street outside the luxury shops. These merchant beggars, these invalids sitting on the pavements where they had chalked out sketches of ships under sail or sunsets over the snow all had a resigned attitude which reminded one of those old paintings where saints await their torture.

When November arrived, blanketed in a sort of dirty yellow cotton wool, Joan dreamed of the blue sky of Sydney, and one morning when she saw two white swans drifting on the muddy coloured Thames near Victoria Bridge, she felt a crazy urge to call out a formidable *cooee* to Jock.

Of all the neighbourhoods of London, the Strand seemed to her the least foreign, for the various states of Australia had their information bureaux there with their window displays attracting passers-by. The Queensland agency displayed samples of minerals, large stuffed fish, and black opals. A little further on, on the other side of the street, Western Australia laid out a wall of pearl shells; further on still, the states of Victoria and New South Wales exhibited fruits, grains, timbers and woollen fleeces that defied the London soot in their glass cages.

Joan often stopped to look at these displays and, contemplating a badly stuffed kangaroo from New South Wales, she might even feel a fleeting moment of gladness.

She was broad-minded; she willingly admired anything that was worthy of admiration. She knew quite well that the Hyde Park in London was not the same thing as the Hyde Park in Sydney; nevertheless, her heart was still back there and nothing in the world would have altered her loyalty to good old Australia. Absent loved ones were always with her, especially when she felt some happiness which she could share with them.

She always kept in her room a triple frame which held the photos of Doctor Kirving and the two MacGillies, father and son. It had been very difficult to get Old Mac to pose for the camera. But for Joan's sake he had braved the lens for the first time in his life.

Joan and her aunt went to Scotland to visit the cottage where Dad had been born. In this land of granite skies and walls, they found a cheerfulness which was both boisterous and hospitable. Strangers had inhabited for a long while the small cottage in Hawick; but once they found out the aim of their visit they willingly let them into the house.

Joan, moved and her eyes glistening with tears, touched the rough surfaces of the walls, caressed the door latches made shiny with use and took note of the sound that they made when they were closed: it was this dry and definite little click that had bade her father farewell all those years ago.

The kind old woman who lived in the cottage was waiting for Joan in the little garden, holding some flowers that she had picked for her, the last of the season, still dripping from the 'Scotch mist' which strangely resembled a fine rain.

For Jock, the weeks at college passed by monotonously. The *Flying Fish* was taken out when weather permitted; but the three men on board felt that the crew was not complete; their little excursions were not so merry.

"I am the last of the idiots," said Doctor Kirving one day, "I have only one daughter and I send her away to the other side of the world. During that time, I grow steadily older, all alone."

"And I," said MacGillie, "I want my boy to go and see the 'old country' one day, but it will have to be later. First he is going to finish college and learn how to make sweets, like his papa. It's a clean trade, it's decent and it makes money."

Jock left behind his studies with regret, anxious after all to commence his apprenticeship as soon as possible, at the factory as well as in the office.

The first week spent manufacturing MacGillie products delivered him for the rest of life from the temptation to eat sugary things. The atmosphere, by turns chocolate, caramel, or mint, when it was not all three at once, seemed disgusting to him at first. Gradually, however, he became used to it.

He took an interest in the machines which blended the sweet pastes with their slow and patient stirring; then cut them into shapes and wrapped them up with their steel fingers, so nimble and neat. The men and women who oversaw the work were dressed in white. No product was touched by a bare hand: the packers wore gloves to arrange the toffees in their boxes.

Jock felt full of admiration for the old miner who had established this industry; from a small roasting pan of burnt sugar had grown the House of MacGillie. In the office, in the place of honour stood the metal drum pierced by the blows of a pickaxe, the company's original boiler.

"Well, Jock, how's the sugar business going?" asked the doctor one evening.

"It's a sticky business, but it's doing well, thanks, doctor."

Old Mac came to the rescue. "Sugar is no joke, Kirving; it's very useful to your profession; it helps you to get people to swallow your pills and your syrups, and where would you be without them?"

Jock thought constantly of the absent girl; she often sent him her news. The descriptions of outings to the theatre, of weekend excursions on the river often left Jock in a pensive mood. Joan had recently sent her photograph taken by Van Dyck: she already seemed a bit transformed, more womanly; she had changed her hair style. She must have many admirers, thought the young man. For another six months, Jock awaited the letter which would announce Joan's impending return. For her, time was passing, the tea parties, the invitations of all kinds barely left her enough leisure to write a few letters. Several of her admirers had fallen truly in love and had risked certain questions which required an answer as brief as it was categorical. Joan supplied them with a 'No' wrapped up in a rather special smile which implied acknowledgement and sympathy.

In the case of a refusal, the Anglo-Saxon does not consider himself insulted personally; his vanity is not so puerile or foolish as to make him fall out bitterly with the young woman who refuses his hand.

Two of the unlucky candidates came to see Joan off when her boat departed, and filled her cabin with roses. These suitors had not lost all hope, and good-naturedly, for the second time, they heard a decision which was without appeal. They stayed with her until the last minute; they bade her adieu with unconcealed emotion. They left the boat which was wailing its siren, glancing enviously at the young male passengers who were about to make the crossing in the company of the woman they so admired.

The return voyage was long; Joan left behind her all regrets for a sojourn that everyone had made so pleasant for her. Every morning, upon awakening, she felt herself filled with an inexpressible joy as she thought of the moment of disembarking. The line of red ink was advancing so slowly on the chart showing each day's progress, and the Indian Ocean seemed to her to be an expanse of salt water that was too long in the crossing.

On the morning when the boat sailed through the Sydney heads, the harbour appeared more blue and the sky more clear. She cursed the port doctor who finished off a copious breakfast before allowing the six hundred passengers on board to parade before him. She waved her handkerchief like a madwoman when the vessel steamed slowly past the Taronga Park Zoo, where the polar bears seemed to be roaming freely, not far from the Abyssinian lions yawning on their rocky outcrop – which was separated only by a deep ditch from the visitors.

A quarter of an hour later, in the crowd packed onto the quayside, she could make out Dad, Jock and his father, shoulder to shoulder, and she reflected that the wooden wharf on which they were standing held all that was most dear to her in the world.

FOUR

"Come in!"

Jock came into Joan's room; seated at a large table, she was writing a letter on a large-sized sheet of blue tinted paper. Everything in this very personal room showed that she was not fond of merely pretty or cheap things. The furniture was of no fancy style, but it was solid, comfortable, well made from Australian timbers, silky oak and tulip-wood.

On the mantelpiece stood a row of several photographs of men Jock had never seen before. Joan followed his gaze: "I have just unpacked them; which one do you prefer?" He picked them up and studied them one after the other: "I find them all nice, but I don't know which one I would choose."

"That is just what happened with me, Jock; I never had any particular preference." For the forty-eight hours since Joan had come back, Jock had been feeling towards her a certain shyness that he could not explain to himself. In his eyes, she had changed: she had become a woman, more beautiful, she impressed him, she seemed to have acquired a superiority which gave the impression that a distance separated them. Her voice, her intonation were different; her fitted suit from a good London tailor, and even her shoes, had a sober stylishness and obvious good quality.

Suddenly, Jock felt that he was poorly dressed; that his tie was all frayed, his shoes down at heel; he had never had this feeling in Joan's presence. Because of it he had forgotten what he wanted to say; she helped him find his train of thought.

"Well, Jock, are you pleased to see me?"

"Oh! Joan, how we have missed you! Tell me, do you feel very different? Or at least, do we strike you as a bit strange ourselves?"

"No, dear, you are all just the same as I left you. I haven't changed; I have grown up a little, I have even put on some weight, but otherwise it is still the same Joan. Jock, have you something to tell me?"

She looked at him, her large blue eyes gazing into his; she read in them what she had already guessed, and before he could open his mouth, she dragged him out to the terrace beside the water.

"The first day that we saw each other," said Jock, "fate decided that we would go away together to visit our 'Coral Eden'. I have had a chat with Captain Ross, he will take us there for our honeymoon. What do you think?"

Joan thought the idea was terrific; Dad thought so too. He himself would willingly have undertaken a short sea voyage; but just now, it was unthinkable.

MacGillie showed no surprise when he learned of the forthcoming wedding of his son with Joan; and since he generally condensed his thoughts to a very few words, he merely said "God bless you", as if they had just sneezed.

From the very next day, the engaged couple began to make all the necessary arrangements, and no honeymoon trip was ever studied with so much care. In the end, it was more like a small expedition: Ross would land the young couple on an uninhabited island he knew off the coast of Queensland; they would have to organise a month's worth of provisions and some housing that was demountable.

After a long process of designs sketched out, amended or torn up, they ended up with the concept of a sort of light bungalow whose parts could be set up and dismantled like a Meccano set, with the aid of a few nuts and bolts. The flooring was mounted on short stumps; four walls, of which one had a door set into it and another a window, would support a roof of rubberised material. The framework and the interior partitions were made of compressed plywood; the whole thing would be fairly lightweight and quite sturdy. The furnishing would be reduced to the bare essentials.

There was a long list made up of crockery, cooking implements, tins of food, flour, biscuits, tea, coffee, sugar, etc., not forgetting six bottles of cognac that the doctor had added 'for emergencies' and which were, he said, part of the small pharmacy he had made up for them. A twelve-gauge double-barrelled shotgun, and all kinds of fishing tackle, would help to provide game and fish.

The doctor took a great interest in the preparations and enjoyed going over Joan's lists, where his thick blue pencil left traces of his passage, crossing out the shoe polish and replacing it with Bovril.

Ross had given Joan a wolf-hound which had landed in Australia with a pedigree like a prince of royal blood; his ancestors bore the titles of margraves and grand dukes. His given name seemed so imposing and so difficult to pronounce that Joan baptised him simply as Wolf. Wolf was a handsome example of his breed, and at the age of fourteen months, he was already a creature who inspired respect. His intelligence was lively, and Joan maintained that if she had the time, she could make a film star of him. The dog therefore had his place reserved on board the *Matano*, and a crate of Spratt's Dog Food was added to the list of provisions.

Joan and Jock's wedding took place in the simplest manner possible, to the surprise of many people who didn't realise that such a ceremony could be carried out in twenty-three minutes, in private, and without pomp. For the first time in his life, MacGillie wore a top hat: a sacrifice that he willingly made to please his daughter-in-law. The loading of all the crates had been finalised the day before; Captain Ross had promised to keep the secret so that the young married couple could come on board without witnesses or confetti.

The *Matano*, an old steam yacht, was well adapted for navigation in the Pacific; Ross had loaded it with all sorts of cargoes on his voyages, except for foul-smelling copra, which was greasy and often infested with small beetles which overrun boats.

The captain manoeuvred his boat as close as possible to the terrace at *Talanga*; both fathers were there to wish them bon voyage.

They crossed through the heads at sunset, then set a course to the north. On the first days the seas were a bit rough, and if the passengers had not already found their sea legs through the many trips they had taken with the doctor, there would have been complaints on board. Once they had passed Cape Capricorn and entered the waters of the Reef, they encountered a dead calm.

Ross knew the Queensland coast well, its bare, treeless plains, its isolated beaches on which emus, kangaroos, and occasionally herds of half-wild cattle wandered. He had sailed along shores covered with mangrove forests which seemed to have grown up on pilons; from the trunks of these trees he had gathered oysters, which were actually quite good. He had forded creeks, with one eye upstream, where the crocodiles lurked, and one eye on the sea from where sharks sometimes came in. Never, he said, had he felt so sprightly and agile when crossing through a few furlongs of water.

He knew where to find the shipwrecks of various boats that had come to grief on the Great Barrier; one of them, in the vicinity of Cape Palmerston, had long since been an enigma, for nobody knew where it came from. One theory had been put forward that this wreck had been part of La Perouse's flotilla lost at Vanikoro and reconstructed by the survivors of whom all traces had disappeared.

Joan and Jock strained their eyes looking out through the binoculars; the captain had promised them their island for the next day, about noon, if all went well.

"The island I have chosen for you is ideal, made to measure; there is a stream of fresh water, a lagoon where you will find what you need to try out your rifle; as much fish as you like, and acres of coral. What's more, it is well off the regular sea routes; you won't even see the boats pass by."

Ross was not far wrong; they arrived off the island early the next morning, and the rumble of the anchor chain woke up the passengers. Through the open hatches, they could see close by the vegetation growing behind a beach of white sand. They dressed hastily, and after breakfast was over the small launch was lowered into the water and loaded up with all the crates it could carry. Ross wanted to be with the first landing; he sat at the tiller and the rowers plied their oars with their backs turned to the promised land.

The turquoise blue water over the white sandy bottom soon became shallow enough to reveal its magical treasures. Living corals of every colour, from pale violet to dark red, strange sea urchins with long spines, appeared beneath the keel, which seemed to be floating on air, so transparent was the water. Fishes of all sizes, striped like tigers, painted with dazzling colours, darted left and right.

The launch started to scrape the bottom, now covered with dead corals, white, in multiple shapes of shrubs, sponges or corollas of large flowers.

Everyone had put on some old shoes, following the captain's advice; they would have to get out and walk through the water while avoiding the often dangerous scrapings of the corals. Joan and Jock finally landed on the snow white beach, sparkling in the sun.

They stopped before the wall of vegetation as if they were meditating before entering a sacred space; and the pandanus trees with their leaves growing in spirals around their rough-hewn trunks, stirred by the morning breeze, greeted them with a welcoming   rustle.

The captain showed them the way to the freshwater creek, not far away; then, when the crates had been unloaded, he set off back to the yacht to fetch the rest.

The two of them felt a strange, inexpressible joy at knowing that this island would be their world, theirs alone; their paradise. They walked along the beach, feeling like children, and oblivious to everything, soaking up this sun, this breeze; their eyes drank in the blue that the sky and the sea had laid out just for them.

They arrived at the freshwater creek which, before disappearing into the sand, filled up a large pool it had hollowed out in the coral rock. Its sides were smooth, and when they saw this crystal basin, they both had the same idea: in the blink of an eye they undressed and slipped into the pool.

Joan had removed her clothing in a few swift movements, as if she was glad to throw off what was encumbering her. She felt the revelation of a joy that she had wished for all her life. It was the realisation of a dream dormant in her race since forever, since the time when her ancestor lived in the dark forests, dressed only in her long hair as brown as dried ferns and wearing a necklace of bears' teeth hanging between her breasts.

Both of them had this instinct of the primitive, they were happy to feel themselves naked in the midst of nature. They emerged from the water and left it to the sun and the sweet breeze to dry them off. In this heavenly setting, their beautiful nudity seemed natural to them.

They lay down on the sand which was already warm, and their white-dusted bodies gave off a fragrance of coral and dried seaweed. They made love under the wide blue sky, under the sun, a few steps away from the sea, which seemed to be ceaselessly counting out pearls along the shore, not far from the trees whose dark green was casting patches of shade on the incandescent sand. They made love just as the fauns and nymphs once made love in the grand surroundings of nature, with a love that knew neither fear nor shame.

They came out of their dream and got dressed as they noticed the launch coming back with a fresh cargo. They began to think about choosing the place where they would build their little cabin.

They marked out a spot not far from the creek, near a clump of trees, and helped the captain and the men to bring up the crates and then to erect the dwelling. Everything had been carefully numbered; in a short half hour their house was set up and its only door was mounted nice and plumb. Jock and Joan decided to take on themselves the installation of the furniture and the unpacking of the provisions; perhaps they were eager to be all alone on their island.

"In a month's time, to the day, I will be back," Ross told them as he shook hands with them; "I hope you will not be missing Sydney before my return. Good luck."

"I am not sure," said Jock, "that one month here will be enough for us, captain: bring some more provisions with you, in case we wish to prolong our stay."

The captain promised, with a little smile; Joan thought it was a good idea.

They watched the launch set off from the beach, saw the steam yacht raise anchor and move off after farewelling them with long blasts of the siren.

They waved goodbye but kept silent; only Wolf responded with some long barking, and then he resumed running about like a mad thing on the sand.

The small dinghy that the captain had left with them now became their only possible link with the world, a cockleshell that would allow them, if necessary, to reach the coast about ten miles away. Jock hauled the boat up onto the sand, promising himself to build a shelter for it as soon as possible.

They had to think about taking up residence; the camp beds, the table and chairs were quickly in place; the crates of provisions with their hinged tops became cupboards, since they had been fitted with shelves.

With four poles and a piece of stretched canvas, Jock set up the outdoor kitchen, and constructed a fireplace with stones that were close at hand. A tree near the cabin served as a hitching post and took on the chain designed to resist the strenuous efforts of Wolf.

The bathroom, situated beside the creek, was unique of its kind: three posts, cut by Jock, supported a tin washbasin; one of them was embellished with a sardine tin which held the soap.

Proud of his set-up, Jock called out to Joan: "Talk about modern comforts in your palatial hotels! Look at that! Running water night and day, no extra charge for baths, no chamber maid or valet. No concierge or porter or others who work incognito and who all want to shake your hand at the time of departure."

Joan found it all perfect; but she had just made a terrible discovery when unpacking the household utensils: they had forgotten to bring serviette rings. Jock promised to make some with some bits of creepers or pieces of string; nevertheless, he laughed with surprise that Joan could have forgotten something on her list.

Their first meal still came from the other side of the world; there were some eggs that Ross had left them, and Joan was able to show Jock that she had taken some cooking lessons in South Kensington.

"The good woman who taught us the art of making sandwiches with lettuce leaves, soup without any meat, and mock turtle with some calf's head, often told us that a wife can keep her husband at home by serving him well-cooked food; she herself cooked admirably well, but she had remained an old maid. However, I think she was right. As I passed through certain parts of London, I saw workmen's wives gossiping on the doorsteps and in the streets instead of taking care of the household chores; cold meals, and four times a week the same piece of plain beef served up, isn't that enough to explain why the working man sometimes forgets that you should never strike a woman, not even with a flower?"

Night had fallen, and with it came a calm that weighed gently, like a hand resting on your brow. Small waves spent themselves on the sand with a sound resembling a whisper; the two silent lovers gazed at the metallic surface of the sea, the dark curtain of trees, and the sky hanging over them like a grand imperial cloak.

"Joan," said Jock softly, "what a dream it is to be able to make love in such a grand palace, in divine solitude, in an atmosphere perfumed by both the flowers of the sea and those of the earth"

Later that night they went back into their little house which smelt of resinous pine like a new toy.

The next day, the man got up first to relight the fire and heat some water; then he went off to plunge into the pool and set up the fish traps.

Joan found that the swimming costume greatly simplified life: but she reflected on what women would do if the fashion for clothing was suppressed once and for all; many of them would find that their existence had no meaning. The fashion for nudity would not last. People would start once again to put feathers and flowers in their hair, to adorn themselves with tattoos and animal skins and they would soon get back to where they started.

As soon as breakfast was over, Jock and Joan put on some espadrilles and explored the outskirts of the island that were gradually being revealed by the receding tide.

Before them, the Garden of their dreams was laid out in all its splendour, its mysterious and unsettling variety. At first it was like a mass of great alien flowers, green and red; enormous mushrooms, yellow edged with brown, the whole forming an islet several yards in diameter. Further out, three banks of living coral emerged from the water in long parallel strips which looked like clumps of heather of the most beautiful lilac colour.

Joan and Jock advanced very carefully over beds of coral which, under eighteen inches of crystal clear water, displayed pale pinks, strong reds or dark browns. They would stop every few feet to examine small underwater chasms where delicate algae and sea anemones were growing.

Fishes glided slowly by, vividly coloured, striped and spotted like oriental carpets; some of them had green scales edged with crimson, others a blue body bordered with yellow, or with maze-like striations, or black with two sky blue stripes. Never had soldiers, jockeys or clowns displayed so much variety and originality in their costumes.

For a long time they stood looking over this ditch which had turned into an aquarium; in some dark corners, things stirred, vague, undefined; fish which resembled lumps of rock or big shells covered with marine plants.

They passed over a field of dead corals, resembling a clump of miniature shrubs covered in frost; they saw great skulls, huge sponges, dead white trees, all sparkling in the sunlight.

These little islets were emerging everywhere, while the sea bottom was carpeted with something like cauliflowers of all shades. Right at the bottom they could make out a fat sea slug, the famous *bêche de mer*, or trepang, that the Chinese are so fond of.

Jock and Joan returned to camp along the shoreline; in a small cove they found a pile of timbers heaped up by a high tide: the wreckage of a boat. Here and there were some low cliffs which dropped straight down onto the beach, and their steep surfaces were covered by long strands of blue convolvulus drooping down onto the sand.

An impatient Wolf was waiting for them at the end of his chain; Jock freed him and they both watched him jumping wildly about.

During lunch they talked about 'their island' and how it had given them more than what they were expecting; that was their first impression.

"It's a shame that we are what is called civilised," said Jock pouring some tea; "with some books, and no newspapers, we could live here very well for months."

"In Europe," said Joan, "I saw people who seemed to have barely enough to subsist on; who suffered from the cold, because in that part of the world you must pay to warm your body in winter. I thought then of our own Australia; it is not the Promised Land; we have our own scourges: the rabbits, the politicians and the well-known racing identities; the number of strikes is something chronic. We have our poverty; but it is mostly as a result of drink or idleness.

"But how I would prefer to live in a tent, six feet by twelve, in 'Old Man's Plain' or on our island, rather than drag my wet shoes around on the granite of London or the asphalt of Paris. If all those people realised that you could live here without killing yourself with work, that the sun would keep you warm for eight months of the year, and that outside of the cities wood costs you nothing, would they exchange their pavement or their gutters, their cold park bench or their filthy hovels for the canvas tent, the Good Lord's fresh air and his sunshine? Who knows?

"You talk about civilisation," she continued, "you should hear my father once he has got onto his favourite hobby-horse, carrying on about civilisation with a small c. According to him, the cause of all that is the shortness of life. That's the starting point. Mankind has deplored that since the beginning; then it has decided that the only way to get more benefit out of existing is to gain more time by reducing distances; to reach a maximum of pleasure with a minimum of effort. In a word, one of the most powerful elements driving civilisation is laziness.

"Man's first concerns were hunger, which he tried to satisfy through hunting and farming, and defending his family against the attacks of men or animals. He extended the reach of his arm by increasing his strength; he hurled stones, thus reducing the distance he would have to run to kill a wild pig. Then he invented the spear, the javelin, the arrow, each time able to strike further, with less effort. Meanwhile, his wife discovered that a gourd could hold more water than her two hands joined together, and could reduce the fatigue of going so often to the river. She invented the net, the basket in which she could carry enough roots and berries for two days.

"Man continued to reduce his efforts and act more quickly; the alphabet spread his words through the eye which is more rapid than the ear, distances were reduced by signals given by conch shells, smoke or beacons. Later on, the canoe, the horse, the carriage brought him bit by bit to this obsession with speed which predominates now. He increased the range of his vision, the range of his hearing, and since life seemed to be getting shorter each day for him, he tried to reduce the hour to a second.

"Here, Dad would stop and ask those who were listening: What's next? We have found the means of killing microbes, surgeons have succeeded in repairing men and making them like new; during all this time, artillery has been making marvellous progress, it can butcher entire companies in a trice, and chemistry can boast of smothering a whole town like a nest of wasps.

"And Dad, who is kindness itself, says he believes the Good Lord is so disgusted with his creation that he no longer wishes to have anything to do with it."

In the afternoon, when the tide had risen, Jock took the dinghy out to sea to try out the fishing lines; the catch was abundant. Jock threw back a few fish which were as brightly coloured as parrots; Ross had warned him against certain species that were dangerous to eat. Naturally, the evening meal seemed exquisite to them; the new aluminium frypan sang a song very sweet to their ears.

"Jock," said Joan suddenly, while he was lighting his pipe, "do you know we have not seen a newspaper for a week? Don't you miss it?"

Jock shook his head: "No, I can do without it very well. Politics, the whole world over, is like a dreary mould growing on everything; the other news items have no novelty, even if the latest means of locomotion have offered something new. Despite all that, if Ross brings us a bundle of newspapers, we will read them ... out of habit"

They hastily did the washing up, for they both thought that the night was too beautiful, and that washing up was one of the meanest jobs that had been imposed on humanity.

Joan, used to keeping house at home, and to making many of her clothes herself, had felt from the beginning, like Jock as it happened, that they should assign certain tasks to each other in order to keep body and mind on the go. Fishing, gathering wood for the cooking, would not take up all their time; with the few tools that Jock had brought with him, they began to clear the ground around their cabin, removing the undergrowth and opening up the view of the fine trees. Wolf, too, seemed to want to get some exercise, for he ran energetically up and down the shoreline, bringing back to his masters pieces of driftwood thrown up by the waves. But his favourite occupation was digging ditches in which he would take delight in lying down, his body pleasantly cooled by the sand which had not yet been reached by the sun. Each day, he dug a new trench for his siesta.

During the first week, Joan had accompanied Jock on all his excursions; but he left her alone one morning to go fishing off the reefs, while she had taken on the task of tidying up the surrounds of the cabin. Neither of them had yet seen any snakes; but some rustling sounds heard that morning among the dead branches had convinced her to carry out this work without delay.

Wolf was by her side, she felt a real companionship in his presence, complete security; being alone, on this island, held no terrors for her; no black men nor white men had landed on this shore, which had little to attract them. Across the water, in Queensland, there was a cattle station located twenty miles inland, and that coast, with its inhospitable appearance, was scarcely more populated.

Joan had found that solitude had a strange way of populating the mind, and seemed to attract around her all sorts of presences. The intense life of cities, the constant hum of noisy humanity, all of that distracted the mind and prevented thoughts from flowing naturally like a stream carried along by the gentle slope of its bed. But as soon as solitude descended like a curtain cutting you off from the rest of the world, memory came out of its slumber, called up the imagination and the two of them caused a film to roll before your eyes which did not cease its unwinding.

Now she could understand the madness which gripped solitary people, people forced to watch the same scenes unroll before their eyes for days and months. Their imagination became a narrow cage in which they went round and round like the poor dazed bear in a menagerie.

FIVE

The two exiles were getting to know their little kingdom very well; they had explored it in the company of Wolf, who had frightened all the wildlife of pigeons, blue turtledoves and little red and yellow 'sunbirds'. White ibis, egrets and cranes were flushed out; and along the shore a white-headed sea eagle was fishing. Shouldering his shotgun, Jock would observe and follow their flights; but the weapon remained on his shoulder, he had no desire to make a kill. The island was quite hilly; they walked upstream along the small freshwater creek which led them to a wild gorge in which the tops of some palm trees rose out of a tangle of tropical vegetation. They recognised the red hibiscus, the mimosas, several varieties of eucalyptus and the tree ferns. Vines as thick as cables were tangled together everywhere; the 'lawyer vine' with its hooked thorns formed an impenetrable barrier.

Another time, they were walking beside a small forest of mangroves growing out of the mud when they came upon a thicket of young trees which had grown so densely that they could only just worm their way between the trunks. The ground was still soft and the trace of their footsteps formed a track that was easy to find again on the way back. The air had become stifling in this tangle of trees; the sunlight filtered through the branches seemed to be falling through a misted up window. From time to time they would come upon a clearing in the middle of which stood a tall tree which seemed to be watching over all this young vegetation.

Jock and Joan sat down and put Wolf on the leash so as to force him to lie down; the noise of their progress, rustling foliage and snapping branches, had prevented them from hearing what they wanted to gather up into their ears: the silence.

The long tapering eucalyptus leaves were barely quivering, an absolute calm reigned all around them. It was a heavy calm, a strange silence as if all of nature had stopped breathing. This absence of any sign of life gave them the sensation of being in a sacred grove. They remained seated for a long time on an old tree trunk, daring to speak only in a whisper.

"Jock," said Joan, "how loudly you can hear your own heart

beating! No temple, no church has ever seemed so sanctified as this forest; no set of organ pipes has ever sounded out a hymn as beautiful as the sound of this silence. It is majestic, it is grandiose and beautiful like the ermine mantle that the Good Lord might wear."

Jock, who had never been very good at expressing emotions, had to content himself with clasping Joan to him in a bear-like embrace and pressing his lips upon hers.

Suddenly a sound shattered their ears as if a titan's whip had lashed the sky above their heads, while a black cloud passed over like a lightning flash, projecting a fleeting shadow on them.

"Ducks," said Jock.

They stood up, and one behind the other, continued on their way through the tightly packed trunks of the young trees. They soon arrived at the edge of a lagoon, halted and crouched down so as not to frighten the masses of birds frolicking about on the water.

The ducks literally turned the surface of the water black; pearl-grey cranes, ibis and spoonbills were exploring the muddy edges.

Wolf, always interested, had nevertheless understood that neither his voice nor his agility was required; he kept his silence and only his ears and his eyes were moving.

Such a sight represented the dream of every hunter; Jock did not even consider slipping two cartridges into his gun; Joan was grateful to him for it. When they had had their fill of gazing at this scene, they both understood the emotions of a hunter lying in wait, but in this case they were trying to leave the lagoon without setting off an alarm, without frightening away this small world of birds which seemed to be the inviolable guests of a sacred pond belonging to some temple hidden in the jungle.

They made their way back following their own tracks; and it was only when they were out of the woods that they spoke in their natural voice and gave Wolf his freedom.

"We won't be eating duck again this evening," said Jock. "I could never have fired a shot into all those feathers."

"No," added Joan; "this evening, the menu will be grilled fish and rice with molasses. It will be easy to prepare."

Jock had given himself a new task, and the next day he set resolutely to work as soon as he obtained a promise from Joan not to come near where he going to be working. His plan was to block the creek at the very point where it emptied into the pool, in such a way as to make it sing. He had already chosen the quarry from where he would extract rocks of coral which were not too heavy for a single man. He stripped off to work more easily, and loaded the rocks one by one on his shoulder which was protected by a sack. He had soon constructed a low horseshoe-shaped barrage; to his great joy, the water built up and when it began to overflow, he could hear its song. He waited until the water stirred up by his efforts became clear again and he gazed at the silver curve falling into the pool.

He sounded a *cooee* which summoned Joan; she joined him without delay, and when she had admired his work, they tried out the shower and found it delightful.

Both of them had lost all notion of time, and that evening, suddenly, Jock thought of the calendar. In the crate which contained the old food tins, among the brands of French sardines, Canadian salmon or Chicago bully-beef, he found nine empty cans which had contained condensed milk; he made a calculation: one every two days. He let out a cry of amazement and said to Joan: "Eighteen days we've been here; is that possible?"

She repeated "Eighteen days?" with an incredulous air.

"In that case," said Jock, totally disgusted, "in twelve days' time we are going to have to pack up our trunks and put our clothes back on; are we going to wear shoes and stiff collars? Do we have to disguise ourselves and re-enter what is called society?"

"Impossible," said Joan, "we are not ready; we have not yet had time to find our feet properly in this paradise."

And that night, while the new moon, delicately balanced on one of its points, seemed to be performing a circus act in front of the multitude of stars, Joan and Jock decided that the steam yacht would be sent back to Sydney, unless there was an absolute need for their presence back there.

Two days later, Jock awakened his companion by wishing her a happy birthday. He had not forgotten Joan's anniversary; the tins of Nestle's milk had certainly refreshed his memory. She opened the wrapped parcels with the impatience of a child and found in them a complete trousseau ... for a desert island: a bathing costume, black with a single white stripe, a pair of espadrilles, a Japanese parasol made of oiled paper, and a plain gold bracelet which Jock slipped on to her just above the elbow. Everything suited her; and the Japanese parasol surrounded her with a glowing aura which played in her hair and brightened up the colour of her skin and her bare shoulders.

A few leaves and some strands of blue convolvulus decorated the small folding breakfast table which saw its menu upgraded with some tinned asparagus and a birthday cake that Jock had ordered in Sydney.

The life of the two islanders was far from being a life of idleness; for, if the household chores had been reduced to the bare essentials, the daily fishing trips took up a good portion of the day. The dinghy often had to be towed quite a long way in order to avoid the corals.

The solitude was even more imposing on a flat sea that was like a sheet of crystal: the transparency of the deep water often caused a sort of vertigo in places where the white sandy bottom would have allowed passage to the keel of large steamships. Leaning over so far as to risk capsizing the boat, they never tired of looking at these strange marine groups moving about in a liquid so pure that it seemed to be a new element made of solid air.

Small silver fish with dark brown stripes, looking as though they had been grilled already, manoeuvred in well disciplined armies, making right and left turns with the precision of a quadrille. A parrot fish, no doubt all by itself so that it could be admired all the better, obligingly showed off its scales, royal blue on a gold background, and its sky blue incisors which formed a sharp, hooked beak. Their field of vision was traversed by the slow sinuous passage of a sea snake, a long viper striped in yellow and brown, with a flattened tail like that of an eel; its bite was just as venomous, they knew, as that of its terrestrial cousins.

Jock, who had his fishing line coiled around one of the dinghy's rowlocks, suddenly felt a tug, then a stronger one. To their great astonishment, the small boat began to move forward, towed by the beast that was at the end of the line stretched to breaking point. Jock managed to make fast his forward rope; he let the fish go where it wanted, for they were in deep, open water.

A king fish, Jock had guessed. They allowed the captive that they had barely noticed to tire itself out as it pleased. The dinghy zigzagged about like a lunatic for twenty minutes; then the struggle seemed to let up as Jock gradually took up the slack and pulled in his line. The roles were soon reversed, and the king fish was towed up to the beach where Jock put an end to its struggles with a well-placed knife blow to the base of the skull. Joan set off to the camp to fetch a rope with which they dragged the beast along the sand.

The fish weighed between 90 and 100 pounds; fortunately, they had a good supply of salt, and after taking two good cuts for their dinner, they were able to salt the rest and sleep with no worries about the next day.

One morning, the discovery of a large turtle gave them a new distraction; she had just laid her eggs in a hole that she had filled in with sand, and was getting ready to go back to the water when Jock caught sight of her. He ran with all his might and turned her over on her back. The turtle, with her flippers waving vainly in the air, looked like a huge cockchafer that had fallen out of chestnut tree; Joan looked with pity at the mummified head and the terrified eyes; Wolf circled around her a few times, keeping clear of the large flippers.

"It's good, turtle," said Joan, "Dad maintains that it is like beef that tastes slightly of fish; but Jock, we are not going to eat her."

Jock was not hard to convince, he had no intention of killing the poor creature. So he turned her on her side, put her back on her feet, and they both watched with pleasure as the turtle took to the water, leaving behind on the sand the deep furrows of her passage.

"What great Robinson Crusoes we are," said Jock with a laugh; "we refuse to shoot ducks, we play heads or tails with a turtle, then we set her free. Are we perhaps too gentle with animals? And yet, when it comes to a poor snagged fish, we make it suffer because of our fish hook, we let it asphyxiate in the bottom of our boat with the very fixed idea that fish don't feel anything. As for the poor worms, we all know that they only wriggle to get some exercise."

The following morning, Joan realised that it must be about Monday, the day of the week which, the world over, seemed to be devoted to the family washing. She put on an apron, no doubt to avoid getting her bathing costume wet, and started cutting up a bar of soap with some string.

Jock had gone out to look for some planks among the boat wreckage, thinking that Ross might perhaps be glad to have them on board.

She set herself up beside the pool, and kneeling over the water, began her task. Rarely could a washerwoman be so distracted by such a setting: the beach formed a gentle curve up to the promontory; as the tide went out, under the great dazzling sun, the white corals began to break through the surface of the water with their shrubs of all shapes.

The washing itself, composed mainly of bath towels, a few handkerchiefs and several kitchen cloths, was quickly done; floating unpretentiously in the breeze, it would have made millions of housewives jealous. Joan could not prevent a smile as she looked over her display of flags. It was good, this simple life.

The crate containing their little library had not often been opened; they had had so much to say to each other, so much to look at, to discuss, that they didn't feel the need for reading matter. Each night, they were tired with the good tiredness of their body, and the lantern which they had brought was hardly ever lit.

They often looked out in a southerly direction, with the fear always present of seeing some smoke soil this horizon that they were starting to consider as belonging to them. Ross had stated the truth, boats did not come close to their island.

Their island: they now felt they knew it as well as their own home; they had made a complete tour of the shore, and had noted with pleasure that no humans had left any traces of their passage: no empty bottles, food tins or oil cans glinted in the sun, no obvious evidence of civilisation.

It was only the ships' wreckage piled up in the rocky cove that evoked the idea of mankind; and many were the theories and suppositions about these things which came to Joan's and Jock's imagination. This wooden flotsam thrown up by the tide like a handful of matches could have filled up a whole volume: ghost ship? shipwreck? mutiny? Anything seemed possible.

The sea, which is said to be so changeable, is the only thing in the world that has not altered since the creation; it has kept its mystery; its fauna, richer and more strange even than that on land, is largely unknown, as is its flora. With all its beauty lit up by the sun, with its comforting placidity, it maintains all the terror of its depths, as dark and mysterious as eternity.

SIX

The steam yacht was due to arrive the next day; on the next day, perhaps, the dream would be over. Thinking about it, Joan and Jock remained silent. This month had flowed by so quickly, like water in the little creek, so calmly, and with the cheerfulness of a song. Both of them felt a struggle going on inside them; they wanted to be once more with those who were dear to them, and at the same time they dreaded to tear themselves away from this existence which had gathered them into its embrace, at once gentle and strong.

They had abandoned their clothes with such relief and joy, and had rejected wearing shoes as being the heavy, clinging sediment of civilisation; and they now hesitated at putting all that back on again.

"All in all," wondered Jock while scraping the scales from a plump silver fish destined for their lunch, "what have we really missed during these last few weeks? Our parents, agreed, and also a few friends; but beyond that?"

"Yes, what else beyond that?" echoed Joan.

"Nothing," said her man, "I can think of nothing. Do you know what society does? It just keeps carrying on."

It was decided therefore that they would only move out at the last possible moment; they would wait to hear the news that Ross would bring, and if all was well, they would send the yacht back.

"Only, if we keep on living like this," said Joan, "we might never wish to leave this little place again ... that is why I haven't wanted to plant anything, no flowers or vegetables."

"There is no danger of that, unfortunately," said Jock; "sooner or later we would be driven mad by the desire to see once more the smoking chimneys, the rumbling trams, the baying automobiles and the shops which sell heaps of indispensable things which we have done without for a month."

Just to be safe, they drew up an inventory of the stores: there was enough to eat for two weeks if necessary. That night, before going to sleep, they each confessed that they had no wish to leave the little island that had become so dear to them.

Early the next morning they were out in the dinghy; they wanted to show the captain what they were capable of and they were hoping for a good catch. Wolf was with them, although the small boat did not have much room for three, and the dog's liveliness occasionally threatened the vessel's equilibrium. But the hooking of each fish was too exciting for Wolf, and it was with the greatest difficulty that the two anglers managed to remove their hook from a very frisky prey that the dog wanted for a toy. The fishing was good; they also collected some oysters from the mangroves.

Never had a horizon been so keenly scanned, except perhaps by some poor castaways; the scarcely visible line between sky and sea remained blank, without even a vague smudge of smoke.

The afternoon was already well advanced when they finally saw the yacht, a small dot giving off a puff of steam. When the chain creaked and scraped, when they saw the anchor plunge into the water with a big white splash, Joan suddenly stood up; she went to the little cabin, slipped a light robe on over her bathing costume, and put on some espadrilles. She even applied a bit of face powder, but the small cloud gave her tanned face such a pallid appearance that she wiped it off with a towel.

Jock was at first rather surprised to see her dressed, but then he understood: they were about to receive some visitors.

They waited on the beach; the sound of the approaching oars was a sweet music to their ears. Finally they heard the captain's *cooee*; they replied with a voice that was not their usual one, so great was their excitement.

"All's well," called out Ross, making a megaphone with his hands. Jock repeated: "All's well."

After some warm welcomes, the captain handed them some letters and newspapers, and passed on all the best regards of the doctor and Mr MacGillie; they were both in very good health. "They envy you, and they bet their best hat that you would not be coming back this time."

Ross and his men had brought more supplies; dinner was promising, with a cold leg of lamb, some salad, fruit and some beer. They set the table while Joan and Jock read their mail. These letters all finished with a very important P.S.: "If you really feel like it, stay for one more month in your paradise; it's an opportunity you won't get again in your life. Captain Ross has some supplies for you."

They looked at each other and read the other's thoughts: "Another month, what bliss"

"Captain," said Jock, "you have lost your bet, but you will get your hat just the same; we will not be coming back with you."

"That doesn't particularly surprise me," said Ross. "You have a few newspapers to read; you won't find in them a half-ounce per ton of anything worthwhile: that was about the content of the ore in a gold mine that I used to work in Queensland a long time ago. Nothing changes! In politics, the farce goes on; a grocer, minister for finances, handles them like a sack of coffee with a hole in the bottom; a lawyer-cum-gramophone-cum-megaphone, makes speeches about commerce and agriculture; some individual with dirty fingernails is in charge of health. All those people have one thing in common: they are afflicted with the gift of speech.

"We have right now a new kind of strike in New South Wales, where every type of strike has been tried: the employees of funeral parlours are refusing to work; you can't even die in peace without worrying about the housing crisis.

"In other news? Tsaratolo has won the Five Hundred Guineas at Randwick; Mack Cartney, of Goonoopanda, sold a ram for three thousand seven hundred guineas … They need rain in the Riverina.

"Your papas are both well, they miss you; they envy you, and say that if the patients and the toffees allowed it, they would come and join you. The doctor has no complaints about his profession, and as for MacGillie, he has become a celebrity. All the population of Sydney who don't yet know how to blow their nose can spell his name; they crunch it, they chew it, they get stuck in it. You have there two men who serve humanity in different ways.

"And you, Robinson Crusoes, what do you think of the simple life? I have tasted it for months and months, I know what it's like; on my island I didn't have any condensed milk or tinned asparagus, but I had coconuts, fish and shellfish: I lived through something like three hundred and ninety Fridays without meat in a row.

"Tell me, Joan, what did you miss the most, apart from Dad, of course?"

"I didn't really miss anything," replied the young woman. "One afternoon when it was very hot, I did dream about an iced pineapple juice; another evening when the moon had painted a great silver lake on the sea, and the wind was blowing through the palm trees, I had a desire to hear the overture to *The Flying Dutchman*. But all that was only a trick of the imagination."

"Deep down," added Jock, "we always miss something; come the day when we have all that we desire, life would not be bearable. We must consider the things of this life a bit like Dad's toffees: the kids who can't afford them often love them and dream about them; the ladies who work for MacGillie and Son, they are sick of them ... so are we ... and Dad too.

"To hope without desire, to have ambition without envy, I think that especially is what brings happiness.

"In that case, captain, we have what we need to be happy, because we envy nobody, absolutely nobody. Joan is not jealous of the woman who has a beautiful pearl necklace, the gown of a princess, or the fur coat of an empress; as for me, I have no desire to be the rich man who owns half a dozen automobiles and can afford a ten shilling cigar with his coffee. The happiest man is the one who has enough to live on, and who is satisfied with his lot. We know that there are many unfortunate people in the world, but there are almost as many old grouches who will complain about the drafts in Heaven and ask Saint Peter to close the door. These are the ones who ought to consult Doctor Kirving: it's almost certainly their liver or their stomach."

The captain had brought with him four of his men to the island, glad to offer them a little distraction. Two of them were Australians, and the other two Norwegians. None of them could understand that some people might spend their honeymoon on a desert island, instead of going to the Blue Mountains, or Tasmania or to New Zealand, which are the classic destinations for honeymoons. They did not understand this voluntary exile; a whole month without going to the cinema, the Tivoli or the races, a month without having a good time!

"Well then," asked the captain, "have you made up your mind? You still have two hours, time enough to pack your bags and raise camp."

Ross's shrewd eye met Joan's.

"You must excuse us, Captain, but we are not yet ready to leave our island; we like it so much here. Come back in a month … give us a little more holiday!"

Joan and Jock wrote a few letters; the captain took them after unloading fresh supplies, and they bade each other good-bye.

"I lose my wager," said Ross; "but it's a real treat to see people happy. Good luck to you both, and I'll be seeing you soon."

They watched the launch head off, and when the *Matano* sounded farewell once again, Joan took Jock's hand and squeezed it with all her might.

SEVEN

The island had become part of their existence; they felt that they could never go away from it now. They sketched out plans; they even fantasised about purchasing or leasing this piece of rock that billions of tiny life-forms had caused to emerge from the sea by dying throughout millions and millions of years. They had once again taken a tour of their kingdom, running like children along the beaches, inspecting the coves and inlets; and each day they loved it more. Jock could already envision, on the northern heathland, a plantation of coconut palms and banana trees. Joan dreamed of a bungalow hidden among the trees; she had chosen the location, not far from their little cabin. Nearby there grew two tall trees from which hung those long pods of dark brown beans, as hard as wood, that jewellers in Brisbane and Sydney mounted on silver to make into matchbox cases. A bit further on there was a flame-tree ablaze with all the glory of its bright red flowers, there were tree-ferns, climbing ferns, big spider lilies, and on the branches of trees there were orchids, staghorns with large branching leaves, and mosses of all kinds.

The other garden, the garden of corals, had not yet unveiled all its mysteries to them. They guessed that in its darker corners and its deep crevasses there were terrible struggles, cruel deaths. The crabs were not safe in their armour, the fishes camouflaged themselves as marine plants, or stones; they bore spines whose wound was fatal; there were giant anemones almost two feet in diameter; other smaller ones, hidden among the seaweeds, could inflict stings from which you suffered for a week. Octopuses took on the colours of the rocks, watching out for their prey with their round eyes. A whole world was hiding, lying in wait or on the defensive, a miniature jungle, more treacherous than the jungle of tigers, in the silence of the shady watery depths.

Flowers of every colour, which were animals, opened and closed their petals to swallow up invisible prey. Deeper down, corals formed moorlands scattered with clumps of petrified plants and small shores on which fat bubbles of white froth had crystallised. Everywhere in the transparent water appeared beds of flowers of many colours, mushrooms turned upside down, bowls, goblets, red fans, laces of pink, yellow or blue.

One morning Jock had gone off fishing beyond the small headland which formed the southern horn of the crescent-shaped beach. Joan had wanted to finish off a bath robe that she had fashioned from some terry towels. She had set herself up in the filtered shade of a clump of pandanus trees, seated on one of the empty crates which formed almost all their furniture.

Wolf, stretched out with his nose on his paws and exhaling on the sand with each breath of his semi-sleep, was lying next to her. She hummed as she sewed, raising her eyes from her handiwork to follow the flight of a sea bird, or to watch a wave breaking lazily on the fringe of crushed coral. She had completed her robe and was trying it on with the same movements and pirouettes that she would have executed in front of a mirror at David Jones store in George Street, when she suddenly froze like a shop window mannequin.

Wolf had woken up and was softly growling. A whaleboat had just come around the northern point; it was not Jock, she was sure of that, and his dinghy was much smaller. Her first movement was to put the dog into his collar, while cursing this stranger who was coming to disturb their solitude.

She waited; the boat was coming closer to the beach, and Wolf was barking, for he had caught sight of it when he stood up, pulling on his chain.

The whaleboat looked to be heavy, too wide and too empty for the man who could barely manage the long oars. Joan was beginning to make out a straw hat which had a broad brim overshadowing the face turned towards the land. Just then, the man saw her and made a distress signal. He ceased rowing, and standing with some difficulty, he got out of the boat; in water up to his knees, he staggered among the submerged corals.

Then Joan felt afraid; but she did not move; her only thoughts were of the shotgun which was behind the door, of Wolf who was straining to go and receive this unexpected visitor. But when she saw the man fall to one knee, and then get up again with great effort a few yards from the beach, she forgot her fear, swiftly tied the cord around her bath robe and went over to him.

He watched her with the wide open eyes of a hunted animal, sunk deep in their orbits as if they were hiding from terror. His face was emaciated; the skin stretched tight over the cheekbones, and the jaw was like tanned leather, and bore livid blotches of sea salt. A ten-day-old beard added a wild, ape-like touch to his physiognomy and concealed his chapped lips soiled with dried spittle.

A rough, barely audible voice said: "Water," and the man made a sign for drinking, his thumb touching his mouth. With painful effort, he followed Joan who had beckoned him to come, and his bare feet, cut by the corals, bled in drops on the white sand.

Joan sat the man down in the shade and gave him some water in small sips; she had to use all her strength to prevent him from drinking the contents of the pannikin in one go. She warmed up some Bovril, offered him two broken biscuits, which he gobbled like a hungry beast; then she bathed his feet in permanganate and put on some bandages.

This human wreck was reduced to an animal state; he did not possess the gift of language for now. With a mechanical gesture, the man removed his straw hat to reveal his premature baldness and a sunburnt scalp, red and painful looking.

Then he fell into a brutish sleep, his legs spread wide and stretched out to their full length, his arms outstretched as if he wanted to use all the space offered to his limbs.

Joan gazed at the man, and his face, which did not shed its suffering in sleep, gave her a pang of pity; she regretted her initial reaction of selfishness. She looked again at the hat made from woven vegetable fibre, and fear gripped her. She recognised a matting made from palm leaves, identical to the one that was in her father's smoking room, the present from the hangman of Nou Island, the hat which, since four o'clock on a certain morning, had no more use.

Wolf was still growling; Joan raised her hand and signalled him to be quiet as she slipped away to see whether Jock was coming back. The dinghy was not in sight, and since she noticed that the whaleboat was being gently rocked by the tide which made it dance about like a cork, she went into the water and hauled it up as far as she could onto the wet sand.

The name on the bow had been scratched off with such care that you could see the bare wood; the stern had been treated in the same way. There was almost six inches of water in the bottom of the boat; two straw hats were floating about as well as a dozen coconuts which knocked into each other at the slightest movement with a noise like a wooden cowbell. She also discovered a pair of rough clodhoppers bearing laces made from palm fibres. There could be no doubt: an escapee from New Caledonia. "Where were the others?" Joan wondered. "Dead from hunger, or thirst? Or …" She thought of another reason.

She went back to the cabin; the man was still asleep, spread out as if on a crucifix, as motionless as a cadaver.

An hour of waiting went by. What sort of man was this? A murderer? A common thief? or a forger? She tried in vain to read this face; but exhaustion, suffering and perhaps the proximity of death had marked it so profoundly that it was impossible to guess what its features might be hiding.

Jock came home at last, in a triumphant and merry mood; when Joan, coming to meet him, told him her story, his first word was a *damn!* sending to hell the poor devil who most likely had just come from there.

The sleeping man had not moved. After a lunch eaten in haste, Jock and Joan set off to inspect the whaleboat; Jock emptied out its water so as to see whether any other clues might be found in it. He discovered only a pocket knife decorated on its horn handle with an Eiffel Tower, and a label on which you could still read that the government factory guaranteed that it had confirmed there were sixty Swedish matches contained in the box.

Jock, more and more convinced that he had been chosen by Fate to play the Good Samaritan, was furious and wondered why this same Fate had not conveyed this escapee to some other haven; the Queensland coast was extensive enough. His Christian charity was no more awakened when, on their return, they saw the man still in the same position, immobilised in the posture of the two thieves who probably had not deserved the ultimate torture as much as he did.

But Jock was at the same time too Scottish and too Australian not to think through the practical side of the adventure: he chose a spot on the other side of the creek, at a fair distance from their cabin yet still easy to keep an eye on. Helped by Joan, he carried down to it the planks that he had chosen from the heap of wreckage in the little cove. Before sunset, they had erected a shelter in the shape of a tent, complete with a floor and a frame which would serve as a bed. Some grasses and leaves were quickly formed into a sort of mattress.

They woke the man up, gave him some biscuits and some Bovril, which he accepted without saying a word; Jock helped him to bed down in his hut, leaving some water and a pannikin within his reach. Under the woollen blanket which Joan had given him, the escapee fell back into a deep sleep straightaway.

As they looked up at the beautiful starry sky, Joan and Jock were still shocked by Fate's infernal joke in throwing up this undesirable castaway onto their island. Then they thought about the poor devil who had tried to gain his freedom, man's most cherished possession, without which he is no longer a man. They thought about the terrible privations he had undergone in order to cover the seven or eight hundred miles which separate Nou Island, with its shark-like silhouette, from the coast of Queensland.

They considered what was to come: since the man was unwell, they would care for him as best they could, they would build up his strength with what they had in their small store made of crates stacked one upon the other. Once he had recovered, they couldn't just tell him to get back in his whaleboat and go and get lost somewhere else. Meanwhile, what was to be done with him until the steam yacht came back?

Before going to bed, Jock, armed with his lantern, went off to see how their new lodger was going; loud snoring sounds told him from a distance that all was going well. As she wished Jock good night, Joan said to him: "Darling, we have had our dream in spite of everything; it was shorter than we wished, but we have held it, we have lived it; we shall never forget it."

And he, kissing his companion in the dark, felt a tear suspended from her eye. She had never shed tears in front of him, still possessing that modest strength that had been ingrained in her when she was young, at the time when she would fall over and get up again, with bloodied knee, without complaining, her eyes dry.

It was a while before they went to sleep; Jock, the Bad Samaritan, got up once more in the middle of the night to see if the man needed anything; he had not so much as stirred under his blanket.

At daybreak, Jock relit the fire and made some coffee that he took over to the other side of the creek. The escapee drank it in small mouthfuls as he had been told to; he asked if he might have a cigarette.

Jock came back with a packet of *Three Castles,* and the first puff, greedily inhaled, produced a sudden effect on the man; he seemed to regain at once his use of words and his intelligence.

At college in Sydney, the French language had for long been considered as an extremely dead language; and in spite of a teacher who read aloud the *Contes du Lundi* with an Irish accent acquired in Australia, Jock had learned a few words and a certain number of phrases.

"Are we far away from any town here?" asked the escapee. The answer seemed to please him.

"Where do you come from?" questioned Jock in his turn. The other man looked at his interlocutor, he could see two plain-speaking eyes, which, it was clear, expected only plain speaking in return.

He stated simply that he had come from New Caledonia; eleven days in a whaleboat, with some biscuits, some fresh coconuts and some coconuts filled with fresh water; ... the other two had not been able to hold out; when they ran out of water, the others had drunk sea water, they had gone crazy.

Sitting on a crate that Jock had brought him as a seat, the man was making a broom out of a palm frond; he felt himself being watched and his keen eyes, too close together, knew that they could not bear the gaze of his host.

"You won't shop me to the police?" he ventured.

Jock shook his head: that was the last thing he would have thought of doing. As he moved off, he looked back to see the man, feeble as an old timer, going back into his hut to lie down.

No, he would never give up to the police a poor blighter who had struggled so much, who had had the courage to test fate, knowing that his chances were one out of five. Life on the island was completely disrupted, naturally, even for Wolf, who felt himself watched and chained up like he had never been. As soon as the man had recovered, a problem would present itself: the one about the wolf, the goat and the cabbage. If Jock and Joan went off fishing together, Wolf and the escapee would be left without surveillance; Jock would not leave his wife alone anywhere near the stranger. That complicated everything. On the other hand, leaving the man alone all by himself would not be prudent.

They ate some corned beef, with tinned vegetables and some rice: as evening fell, Jock busied himself fitting the door of their cabin with a padlock that he had borrowed from one of the crates; he hid the cartridges and the shotgun; he buried in the sand the six bottles of cognac which, for the time being, were as dangerous as a shipment of dynamite.

By the end of the first week, the man was taking more solid meals and showing a taste for coffee that was compromising the stock of their little store; the cigarettes had more or less run out, and Louis - that was how he had introduced himself - had received very badly the news of an imminent shortage of *Three Castles*.

Jock had given him a few items of clothing, and he had gratefully accepted a brush and some soap; but the razor was of no interest to him: he was definitely determined to let his beard and moustache grow.

As a result of his growing appetite, he built up his strength and began to go for walks along the sea shore. His face had completely changed during this past week; Joan was the first to be frightened by this sudden metamorphosis which had done away with his look of a hunted animal. The escapee's eyes, now gleaming and more mobile, seemed always on the alert, as if they were looking for something; the fear which had formerly marked them had been replaced by the shiftiness of a cunning animal. His short, shapeless beard gave him a sinister appearance.

The man's curiosity pushed him to ask questions of Joan; he wanted to know where they came from, how they had arrived here, when they were going to leave. Joan gave a vague answer to all that: "We are expecting the steam yacht any day now, so as to return to Sydney."

He often looked in Wolf's direction with a fear mixed with hatred; the dog hated him, as well, but without any fear. He would become talkative, seeming to have the power of persuasion; he would come out with carefully chosen words and ready-made phrases.

"Talking does you good. It was eight years that we spent there," he said, encouraged by a packet of cigarettes that Jock had discovered; "we built roads, cleaned the streets; when we talked, we would whisper, pass the word around, just the odd phrase; we communicated like deaf and dumb people, with signs.

"What did I do to land in New Caledonia? I am not afraid to tell you. I killed a man through jealousy; I deserved some sort of punishment, for sure, but not as much as that."

As he was speaking, his voice got more worked up, he became more like a professional speaker, he took on an attitude as if he was addressing a meeting.

"Justice? That exists no more than perpetual motion does. It is an ideal, nothing more; it does not exist either in man or in nature. Justice? How do they represent it? A tall lady with poor eyesight holding a crooked pair of scales. In reality, this Justice is aware of her impotence, to the extent that she needs accessories to command respect, to put fear into people. She needs wigs, white rabbit fur; robes with broad sleeves that lend themselves to grand gestures. It's funny, but it's one of the rare professions which still feels the need to dress up.

"Justice, don't we know it! We have paid to get to know it."

The man had forgotten about the penal colony; he had once more become what he used to be, the cabinetmaker from the Faubourg Saint-Antoine, a stalwart of the local community meetings, an opponent of the existing order.

"I made a good day's wages in my trade; I could make you some Henri II or some Louis XV knock-offs, anything in the quality merchandise line. And I swear to you that if Henri II or Louis XV could have sat on them they would be completely taken in.

"I was not a bad man, I was about to be engaged to a pretty girl when another man came between us; I hit him a bit too hard, and there you are.

"As for the escape, we worked on that for four months; the most difficult thing was to put some provisions aside; the easiest thing was to get hold of a boat: one belonging to the gendarmes. We took off one night, we had a compass, but none of us three was a sailor. No wind; three hours later our hands were all bleeding; we had to go on all the same. Eleven days and eleven nights on the bench of a whaleboat, that's hard. We couldn't lie down, it was taking in water, not much, but there was always a few inches in the bottom, and we often had to bail out with our shoes."

Jock and Joan let him go on: the man knew he was being listened to; for eight years, in his prison, he had had time to rehearse his speech. He felt himself coming out of the swamp in which he had languished for so long, he had become a free man once more and he was already looking at his audience with more assurance.

Straining at his chain, Wolf experienced both the jealousy of feeling he was neglected, and a hatred for this stranger whose voice he could not hear without growling.

When Louis went back to his hut, Jock came over to pay his respects to the dog as if to excuse himself for his infidelity. He took the dog for a walk on his chain and examined closely the links and the collar itself.

"Just between ourselves," he said to Joan, "if Wolf gets free, the best thing the man can do is jump into his whaleboat and row with all his might."

No convalescence had ever proceeded so quickly. Louis, who, two weeks before, had been thrown up onto the beach like a bunch of seaweed, a starving creature dying of thirst and exhaustion, was now coming and going, whistling, going fishing with Jock. Jock had scarcely any choice; they needed the fish, and he could not leave Louis behind on land, even though he had given him to understand that his presence was not desired around the little cabin.

He was learning French once again with Louis, whose surname was Buffet. Buffet was talkative; he was also a liar, and Jock had noticed some anachronisms and contradictions in his tales. During his captivity, his imagination must have been a great comfort to him, a constantly renewed distraction; however, they still wondered about those two hats found in his boat; and also about this crime of passion, a fine crime to confess, almost a gallant gesture!

Louis spoke about the privations he had suffered on Nou Island, at Camp Brun. "No tobacco, no wine for eight years. Can you imagine that? They deprived us of all those little things which make life worth putting up with." Jock thought of the cognac, and resolved on the spot to find a better hiding place for it.

Louis seemed to have regained full confidence in himself; he admitted to his companion that he was a good shot and that he was quite sure that he could provide some game for them if there was anything with fur or feather around the place. Jock said that fishing was the only thing that interested him, and that sea birds didn't amount to much as game. Jock returned from this first trip in Louis' company with some suspicions about the escapee, which only grew from day to day. The man seemed all the more dangerous because he was intelligent, because he had a lively mind always on the alert. He promised himself to keep a close eye on him, and to put Joan on her guard without alarming her too much. There was still a week to go before the expected arrival of the yacht; they had both been secretly wishing to see its smoke on the horizon; their island now was no longer what it had been. Louis had landed on it like a vile insect on a flower. As soon as he was in a fit state to do some work, Jock had urged him to overhaul his whaleboat, convincing him that it was necessary for his own safety to have it always ready to set out to sea. Despite his lack of enthusiasm at the thought of recommencing his wanderings so soon, the escapee understood nevertheless that it was wise to be prepared for any eventuality.

He scraped the keel, partly filled the boat with water, then covered it with a roof of palm fronds to prevent the sun from causing its joints to come apart.

EIGHT

"That's definitely the end," Joan said sadly one morning as she was putting on for the first time in weeks a skirt and a blouse. "I don't like the way Louis looks me over, even when I am wearing my bathing robe. He has eyes which peel you as if you were an apple."

"I am keeping watch on him," said Jock, who, with his hand to his forehead, was watching Louis as he fished on the nearby reefs.

They both went over to the dinghy, after patting Wolf and making him understand the harsh necessity of staying on the chain to guard the house. They promised him a walk when they came back.

Wolf, very sad, his ears pricked up, adopted a heraldic pose, his liquid brown eyes watching the masters move off. When he had lost sight of them he turned his head towards Louis' hut, then he felt bored. His long chain suspended from a wire stretched between two trees gave him room to move around a little. He had begun to dig holes, and in the middle of the day he had experienced a delicious sensation lying down in these hollows lined with damp sand. He began some new diggings in the shade of the cabin and for a minute his front paws worked away with the energy of a steam shovel. Suddenly his nails encountered some wood. With his ears drooping and his head cocked to one side in the comical attitude of a curious dog, he made another prudent dig with his paw and uncovered a board of wood. He gave up his digging, slid his chain along the wire, and went further off to make a hollow in which he curled up and closed his eyes.

Later in the afternoon, when everyone, including Wolf, was out for a walk, Louis, who loved to nose about, came over to make a close inspection of the cabin and its surroundings. It was locked up with a good padlock and two sturdy hooks, about as effective, Louis thought, as a piece of cardboard neatly inscribed with the message: "Keep Out".

The single small window was covered by an opaque curtain; the man's monkey-like curiosity was only heightened. With pleasure, he saw Wolf's chain hanging inert from the wire; he would have given a lot to see the dog strangled at the end of it.

Dogs, he knew, hated people like him, as if the odour of the penitentiary clung permanently to them. He remembered the day when he had landed at Hienghene, on the coast of New Caledonia, with three Kanaks and two prison officers. They had just spent the night in a whaleboat that had almost foundered in the breakers. It had been a near shipwreck, the hens had drowned in the bottom of the boat and all the baggage was soaked. At five in the morning they had landed near a settler's residence; but he, Louis, had been unable to disembark until the dogs had been chained up.

Yes, he detested Wolf. He had already thought of ways to get rid of him; he had asked Joan for some laudanum to treat his colic, but he had only been able to get some of the English version of the drug which smells of ether. Then he had thought of crushed glass; but it takes too long to have its effect.

He noticed the excavations that the dog had made in the sand; the ground had been turned over like a rabbit warren. In one of the holes he could see the end of a wooden board; he got down on his knees, cleared away some sand and recognised the top of a crate. He read on it: *Hennessy Three Stars,* 12 bottles!

Louis felt the excitement of a pirate who discovers a treasure on a desert island; he enlarged the hole with the same eagerness that Wolf had shown in starting to dig it, using similar actions to those of the animal in his anxious haste. Knowing that the others could return at any moment, he dug away, removed the sand, lifted the crate from the hole, filled it in, and removed all traces of his feet and the deeper marks made by his knees.

Shouldering the crate, he ran off behind the wall of vegetation and hid in a dense thicket of bush. He established with sincere regret that the crate was not full. He had often enough carried crates of a dozen bottles, Noilly Prat or Pernod, with which "The Penitentiary" lubricated its wheels very regularly back in New Caledonia where the aperitif is an institution as immovable as the Central Mountain Range. Right away, he had judged that the crate contained no more than six bottles; now he needed to find out whether it was genuine 'grog' or bleach.

A few blows with a stone brought the treasure to light: only half a dozen, but it was the genuine stuff. The escapee gently brushed the labels, caressed the unopened caps; he could not have felt more happiness if he had been handling doubloons and plunging in his arms up to the elbows. For years, this had been the obsession and the dream for him and his comrades in the Penitentiary. He had known of comrades who had escaped to get hold of a bottle of cheap wine, who had killed "for a drop of something", invented ridiculous schemes to steal any old drink. The prisoners' band which used to play on the Place des Cocotiers had come back on its barge one evening to Nou Island completely drunk, from the cymbals to the oboe; this orgy was only terminated when they discovered the wine and spirits hidden in the horns and tubas.

Louis put one bottle under his shirt, covered up the crate in the thicket, and headed back to his hut, feeling as light as a soap bubble, in a joyful anticipation of the wild time to come, so near, so certain, so real already.

He barely gave himself the time to cook his fish for dinner; he didn't even bake his damper in the embers, he was so keen to get to … dessert. A swift blow applied with the back of a knife removed both the cork and the neck of the bottle at once, and, with his eyes closed, Louis could sniff the nectar.

He poured some cognac into his pannikin, half filling it, and drank a small sip, prudently. He found it full of fire, he was no longer used to it, he felt the burning sensation creeping down his throat and into his stomach like an acid. Like a connoisseur, he analysed the taste and the aroma, and that heat going into his veins; a sweet, all-enveloping mist rose up in his brain. Bit by bit he felt a sinking sensation; he abandoned himself to it as if his muscles were no longer responding to his will.

Now he has the feeling that the past from which he is just emerging is only a bad dream; his eyes are still open and a vision appears before them, Joan in her bathing costume. She goes into the water and beckons him to follow. But he has had enough of this blue water. The sea had stung his eyes, many a time it had drowned the hope he still possessed, forever sprawled out between him and his freedom. It had taken his two companions from him, after first driving them mad with thirst.

First Remy had gone overboard; he had floated for a moment

like a bundle of rags, then he had disappeared bent over double, in the grotesque posture of a man looking for dandelions.

The following day Jules had climbed over the side of the boat; Louis remembered giving him a lot of help with this activity. At least Jules had dived in head first, naturally, as if he knew the way and where he was going. It must be said that he had three bullets in his head. Poor old Julot, he was not a bad chap; but really, there was not enough fresh water for two, and since Louis was the smarter one, he had put himself in charge of the distribution; three coconut shells full of water for him, and for Jules all the salt water of the Pacific.

He made a grimace which was trying to be a smile and poured himself another cognac. A third one, no more. He noticed that the liquid poured slowly, soundlessly, like molten glass; he drank another mouthful and waited, his hand holding onto the pannikin in a grip that was simultaneously fondling and protecting.

He saw once more before him a reproduction, a popular coloured print that had haunted him since he was a child; it represented a Roman feast. Men were reclining around a large table laden with dishes of every kind, watching naked women dancing on the marble tiles strewn with flowers. Slaves were going around, pouring their amphoras of red wine into big silver goblets.

Someone had told him that that was called an orgy. Since then he had dreamed all his life of taking part in an orgy; this idea had haunted him, it had given him the ambition to get rich in order to be invited to such feasts. It had become for him a reason for living, a whip which lashed him for being poor, which inflamed his hatred of the rich. In the meetings at which he spoke, he had thundered against the bourgeoisie, he had denounced the injustice which existed everywhere, nowhere more than in Nature. From the flea to the lion, animals were all devouring each other; the strongest, the most cunning ones grew fat on the others. Men, naturally, did the same thing, the only difference being that physical strength was replaced by intelligence and treachery.

He had tried to get rich by taking a short cut; but he and his gang had been nabbed, and since a concierge had been stabbed to death, the gang had been consigned to New Caledonia.

He had been robbed of eight years of his life, he was going to be compensated as best he could. At the age of twenty-two he put on the canvas overalls and the straw hat, he had his hair and face shaved, and he was decorated with a five-figure identity number, like a bale of cotton unloaded on the dock at Le Havre.

He wanted to forget the sleepless nights when he was being tormented by the mosquitoes and the heat. The coloured print from his youth kept coming back like an obsession; the Romans kept eating in front of him those dishes that he could enumerate in detail, his favourite dishes; and the wines didn't stop flowing into the goblets. The dancers brushed against him as they passed, he could hear the sound of their bare feet gliding over the marble; he could smell the wreaths of flowers that they wore in their hair.

The vision had returned; in his half dream, he was aware that he was free; that he could forget about these cravings, these years of obsession during which his entire being, driven mad by deprivation and excruciating hungers, had stirred up a riot in his mind.

Suddenly the world went dark for him, as if commanded by a whispered "snuff it" when someone heard Cortanelli, the Corsican, coming near, the one who, for fifteen years, had been barking and growling at the prisoners like a cattle dog on the way to the abattoir. He woke up early the next day; but his dreams carried on, and his eyes open to the sun kept following them. A little cognac refreshed his thoughts and suddenly, as if a screen had been slashed in front of him, he saw in strangely clear detail a "job" he could carry out … First, the dog; no chance while he was alive, then the man. After that, it would be easy.

There were still plenty of provisions, he knew; there was enough to keep fishing with for months, plenty of fish, a whaleboat, a dinghy. He would take the woman away to another island or the mainland; Jock had shown him the map when he had explained that they couldn't take him on the yacht. It might last, and it might not. That all seemed easy after all the risks he had run, a tropical island idyll for two, it appealed to him; we'd see what came next.

Another three days until the yacht comes, they had said to him; there was no time to lose, the "job" could begin tonight.

He spent the day fishing, and going over his plan. He rummaged about around the cabin while Jock, Joan and Wolf were off on a walk along the beach.

He heaped up a pile of wood not far from the whaleboat, added some dry grass to it and, when the night was completely dark, set fire to it. Then he got out of the circle of light and went over to hide behind the clump of pandanus which was half way to the cabin. He had only one bullet left in the rusty pistol that he had hidden under his wide flannel binder; he was ready to change tactics if the shot missed.

Jock, drawn by the inexplicable light, thought from a distance that the whaleboat was on fire; instinctively, for the first time since Louis arrived, he took his shotgun under his arm and came down the little track. The shot did not miss: hit at close range, Jock fell in a heap; the escapee grabbed the shotgun, opened it, and, satisfied to see two shiny cartridges, he threw away his useless pistol and climbed up the slope which led to the cabin.

Joan had seen the fire near the whaleboat and had just heard the gunfire; she had come outside holding Wolf on the chain. She saw a shadow approaching, she could make out the dark outline of the rifle's barrel in the darkness. Her voice was a little shaky because of the silence through which the silhouette was coming closer. She called out: "Jock is that you?"

But Wolf's loud barks as he pulled on the chain had already warned her that it was Louis. The escapee with the shotgun? Where was Jock?

Before she could load another thought onto her anxiety, a flash of light blinded her and, amid the deafening explosion, she felt the dog's chain fall slack in her hands; then she saw at her feet Wolf motionless, shot dead.

A harsh, demented voice yelled: "Jock, where are you?" The escapee knew he was master of the situation; he let her run; he watched her disappear into the night, repeating her desperate cries.

He went into the cabin, picked up the lighted lantern and went off to the thicket to look for the crate that he had hidden there. He lined up the bottles on the table, looked for a corkscrew and two glasses, and set himself up as if he was right at home. He felt he needed to have a drink after these last few minutes; it had not taken long, and everything had gone better than he thought it would. The trick of the decoy had worked well; he was proud of it, and the other one had fallen right into his hands.

Joan, used to the darkness, followed the little beaten track in the sand made by their everyday comings and goings ... their own track; near the clump of pandanus trees she found Jock lying on his back.

"Jock, answer me, it's me, Joan." But he was already gone, his heart was no longer beating, and in the light of the stars she could see his eyes wide open like the eyes of the dead who don't understand, who would never understand why the life they had been given was now taken away from them.

How long did she stay lost in the pit of her despair? Half an hour perhaps. Then she heard a voice calling her name: "Jeanne." Her name, in the language of this man ... She did not move. But the voice called out again; heavy as the cry of a vulture, it was becoming threatening. Her instinct told her that it was better to go back; the monster was singing, striking the table with his fist.

Hunched over his glass, the shotgun in easy reach, Louis signalled Joan to sit down; he filled a glass, refilled his own and said: "Now, the drinks are on me, Jeanne, you are at my place, here's to you."

Her glass in hand, she made a sudden decision: she took one sip. She knew that she needed it, and she saw a heavy task before her. She had to drink the toast, and then when the man stood up to try and grab her, she took refuge on the other side of the table. Caught up by the game, he started to chase her; she waited for her moment and grabbed hold of the shotgun the instant Louis went to close the door to stop her from getting out.

When the escapee turned around, he saw the weapon pointing straight at him. Calm, Joan told him: "Sit down." He hesitated, then he obeyed, shrugging his shoulders.

"Fill up your glass."

He snickered and filled up his glass to the brim; he looked at the bottle of cognac, now three quarters empty.

"Now drink it all in one go, or I will shoot you like a dog." Louis made a grimace as if struck with a whip and stared at the woman with her gun raised at him. He drank slowly, but without letting the glass leave his lips; when he had finished, she indicated to him to go outside; she slipped out, always on her guard, and ordered him to go to his hut, and to stay there.

She followed him at a distance to make sure he went back into his hut; then she went to fetch some cartridges, put on the cartridge belt, extinguished the lantern and took it with her. She stayed on the alert, scrutinising every shadow: she had to protect both her dead husband and her own life.

She kept watch all night with dry eyes, kept dry by an effort of will; she needed to keep her vision completely clear to be able to take aim at Louis in the dark.

She was already aware of the immensity of her misfortune; she had not had the time to question reality, to deny what she could not believe. Grief gnawed at her and tightened itself around her poor mind with an iron grip.

The night air was mild, the sea laid out on the beach the shells that it had been trying to crush since the birth of mankind; frogs were croaking in the background and the pandanus trees were rustling their dry fronds as if Jock were still alive. A grain of sand blown away on the wind, a crushed ant, one man less; what was that in the onward march of Nature? Life meant nothing; Death meant nothing. And Grief, shaped by one and the other, was it, too, nothing?

Instead of sending up a prayer, Joan posed a question, her eyes turned to the stars that were still in Jock's gaze: "O dear God, why this terrible punishment? What have we done? Why have you led this brute to us? I do not understand. Have we perhaps been too happy? Have we perhaps loved each other too much? Have we committed a mortal sin by making a small Paradise for ourselves on this Earth?"

She continued to watch over Jock; she got up frequently and examined her surroundings, listening for the slightest noise, her shotgun always at the ready.

At last morning announced itself with a pale glow; the sea coloured itself rose pink, then reached melting point when the sun made its appearance. A new day was beginning, splendid with all the serene beauty of the sky, the sea and the land; and Jock would never awaken.

Then Joan wept all the tears that she had. She saw them fall onto the white sand that they marked like the first hesitant drops of a rainstorm. She let her grief sing its sad song that only the white seagulls could hear.

She covered Jock with a travel rug, then went back to the cabin to prepare herself something to eat. She had no desire for anything; but she was afraid of giving up before the task was accomplished.

She walked past Wolf's sleeping body, his teeth exposed to the sun, his beautiful teeth, white and faithful. His brown eyes, wide open, were still transparent enough to show the gulf of sadness within them. The eyes of a dog, containing all the love and loyalty which fills their brief existence. Joan felt an unknown force compelling her to kneel in front of the inert creature; she took one paw in her hand and held it for a long time. Friend, companion and defender; he had loved right up to his death.

Her sleepless night, sad and full of pain, had made Joan's cheeks hollow and aged her features, still so youthful yesterday. The sun was beginning to assail her from time to time, but she fought back. She ate mechanically.

From the tools they had brought with them, she selected a brand new shovel, still bearing the brightly coloured label of a Birmingham factory.

She called Louis with a long, repeated *cooee*; the man appeared at the door of his hut and indicated that he was coming. He had understood that their roles were strangely reversed for the time being; but he was resigned to use patience and wait for the chance to seize the gun. She could not hold out for much longer, she would need to sleep fairly soon. So, then! The return to reality when he woke up had refreshed his brain and somehow neutralised the effects of yesterday's orgy.

Joan showed him the shovel, and pointed out the spot where she wanted him to dig Jock's grave; it was in the shade of those pandanus trees which, day and night, in the slightest breeze, make their rustling sound with their dried fronds.

Louis hesitated for a moment; but the angle of the shotgun and the look on Joan's face persuaded him to do the work. For all the time he had been condemned to forced labour, he had never got through so much work in so little time.

The woman, her nerves strained, her muscles aching with fatigue, her head heavy, did not take her eyes off the escapee; she expected him to attack at any moment. Her arms were worn out from constantly aiming her weapon, ready to fire; her hand clenching the chestnut rifle butt was sweaty and she had to flex her fingers frequently to avoid cramps. The man had a surly expression and every time their eyes met she would hold her gun more tightly. He had completed the work; Joan had made him extend one end of the grave, for she wanted Wolf to be buried at the feet of his master. With the long-handled shovel on his shoulder, Louis suddenly stared at the horizon, as if he had just seen some smoke or a sail there.

For just a second, Joan turned her head towards the sea; but she saw in an instant, on the white sand, the shadow of the shovel that was coming down on her. At the same time, she stepped to one side and fired. Louis collapsed from a shot to the middle of his chest.

He was killed instantly, she knew; she felt an immense relief, a deliverance which brought her some consolation in her grief. Now she could be alone with her Jock, alone with her mourning. At that moment she became aware of the burden she had just been carrying, as if the world had been pressing her down with all its weight these last twelve hours, while every second she had been haunted by the fear of that brute.

She set about her cruel duty. Under the hot sun, she laid Jock out in this hole in the sand that was deeper than any bottomless pit; then, with Wolf laid at the feet of his master, she filled in the grave.

Louis, dead as he was, did not seem to her to deserve the honours of a burial. Suddenly she remembered a hole that the dog had dug to amuse himself a few days ago. His excavation was deep enough and had enough room for this corpse without a soul; she removed the dead man's hat. She didn't have the strength to carry this cadaver; any contact with it would have horrified her. She dragged it into the hole using Wolf's chain.

While she was completing her horrible task, in a rage, with great shovelfuls of sand, Joan closed her eyes so that she did not have to look any more at this vile, hateful being who was consigned, even into death, with its feet in chains.

Clenching her teeth, she held in the flood of hatred that she would have liked to let pour into the still gaping hole; she also held back the cry of vengeance that she was burning to hurl into the infinitely blue sky, the very brightness of which seemed to be an insult to her grief.

Her strength had given all that it could, she felt it flowing away like the sand in an hour glass; with a final effort of her whole being, she wanted to put an end to this nightmare. She finished levelling the grave, and staggered back to the little cabin, shattered, half crazy, dying of thirst.

She drank her fill of water, then fell onto the camp bed. She slept for twelve hours, without moving, without dreaming, utterly worn out and as if she was deliberately rubbing shoulders with death which had suddenly become so familiar to her.

NINE

The sun was already high over the beaten copper surface of the sea when Joan emerged from her long sleep. She instantly regained consciousness of things here on Earth, as if the burden had not lifted from her shoulders for an instant. She woke up as a widow from the very first second; inhaling, with the fresh morning air, all the horror of this solitude of her soul within the absolute solitude of nature. She lit the fire and prepared herself a meal; hunger was just one more pain.

Jock was dead, and the sea was still singing its same song; Joan recalled the verse that a stranger had written one day in her album:

All over the world
Tears have flowed;
Deep is the Sea
And salty its load.

Why had this man, encountered by chance, written that for her?

On the flank of their little hill could be read the whole story of the triple nightmare. Not far from the cabin was the spot where Wolf had fallen; Death had left its signature on the white sand. Further away, on the track, the ground had been disturbed; a heel had spun around, a hand had grasped the sand firmly as if to hang on to life, a body had fallen in a heap. Death had left its signature there, too.

Further on still, another disturbance; but Death had not wanted to leave its signature. From that point there began a deep furrow leading to the second little summit, as if a heavy reptile had slithered away to hide in its hole.

Joan, armed with her hatchet, cut off some green palm fronds which she placed around Jock's tomb; then, on her knees, she arranged a border made of pieces of coral that she had fetched from the shore.

Her hatred for the escapee seemed to have waned a little: she fashioned two wooden crucifixes, and by sunset each tomb had its own.

That evening, by the light of the lantern, she tidied up the little cabin, she began to pack Jock's things, finding in her contact with them a happiness mixed with painful regrets. Each thing, each item belonging to him held and would forever keep for her some particles of his existence, of his energy, some atoms of his personality, of his thoughts and feelings.

Joan reflected on the vanity of the efforts she was making to keep going. Several times the idea came into her head not to leave the island, to stay with her dead husband; and this idea bore with it, barely disguised, the desire to go to sleep forever so as not to think, not to remember; not to suffer any more. Why should she keep on marching along the highway of life, alone, without Jock at her side! It would be so easy to let yourself slip gently into nothingness, to go to sleep forever on the warm sand, in a bed made next to his?

On three occasions, she was assailed by the same vision; she went so far as to think the act through calmly, to excuse it, prepare for it; but she believed she heard Jock's voice say to her: "No, don't do that."

He was right; he had been brave, that boy at Coogee; he would never have contemplated suicide. At the thought of her father, of Jock's father, she strengthened her resistance; after all, perhaps the future might give her, as compensation, another life to pamper, to love as she had cherished Jock? She would keep fighting. Those poor parents whom she would have to encounter alone, on her return; she was already suffering from the grief that she was preparing for them.

The yacht was supposed to arrive the next day; one more day, one more night; an eternity of solitude. Nevertheless, she knew that she would be sorry to leave the island behind; everything here spoke to her of Jock. The creek sang a song that he had composed himself, the sand still showed, here and there, the trace of his bare feet; the dinghy, neglected, was waiting under its little roof of palm fronds.

She went once more to bathe in the natural pool that he had discovered between the ramparts of rock that barred entry to the sharks. Before diving in, she gazed into the deep water, of a dream-like blue, of chrysoprase made paler still by the white coral bottom that the sun peered at through two layers of crystal. Once again she contemplated the undersea garden where sea plants grew, long and undulating like the hair of mermaids. Small violet fishes, striped with black, their shape resembling an axe head, swam by like intangible shadows and disappeared into dark crevices. Anemones, marguerites and chrysanthemums seemed to abandon their petals to the slow swell of the sea.

She swam and found in the refreshing coolness of the water a caress that was both soothing and stimulating. For a long while she gazed out at the horizon, while the sun dried her naked body.

Joan sought out things to keep her busy, to still her thoughts and chase them away when they came back on the attack. She continued to get ready for the departure. Through misty eyes, she could see one by one her dresses, bright and gay as spring sunshine; light dresses scattered with flowers, made to soak up the joy of living.

Should she wear mourning for Jock? Her heart was mourning more than enough. She had never understood why you should deck yourself in the outward signs of a suffering so sacred and intimate. To show off one's sorrow to the eyes of the indifferent, to display publicly everything that one's grief sought to keep for itself, that for her was begging for sympathy, fishing for condolences. She found in one of Jock's jackets enough black lining fabric to make an arm band and a band for her hat … Tomorrow, Captain Ross would understand as soon as he saw her.

Several times she passed by the cross under which Louis rested, and not once did she feel the slightest remorse about him. She recalled that when she was a young girl, once, in a small town in New South Wales, she had killed a snake which had crossed her path, a red-bellied black snake, a very venomous species. She had been lucky enough to break its back with the first blow, after which she had crushed its head with savage energy. Killing Louis had been nothing more for her; she knew she had seized the only way to save herself: destroy the beast.

The next day she was ready; the little cabin, still standing, only remained to be dismantled. She set off towards the headland from where the view extended southwards; her eyes, already tired, started to go cloudy from too much scanning of the horizon with the binoculars.

Finally, after midday, the yacht appeared. Her excitement was such that she had to sit down on a rock, and the old pain came back to gnaw at her heart; the idea of leaving Jock behind, of leaving "their" island; this piece of sandy terrain that had seen the happiest days of their lives, and the most tragically sad hours that a human being had ever lived through!

The *Matano* grew slowly bigger as Joan watched; occasionally it even seemed to come to a stop, as if hesitating and trying to find its way through the corals. Several minutes later, she saw a puff of smoke then heard the explosion of the small cannon on board. This jovial and noisy greeting offended her, she was slow to respond, then, standing up, she waved her handkerchief while the breeze spread two tears over her thin, tanned cheeks.

After that, the wait felt long and painful; she heard the anchor chain, she saw the launch being lowered from its hangers and the oars standing upright in a movement like the waving of a beetle's legs when it has fallen on its back.

She was standing next to the water, and Ross was already sending out in his jolly sailor's voice all sorts of questions which were only the impatient expression of his gladness to be back. Joan only waved in return; her voice had got stuck in her throat.

Suddenly, the captain saw the black whaleboat washed up on the beach like a dead whale, and then he noticed the arm band that Joan was wearing on her white sleeve, and the band on her hat. He realised that some misfortune had occurred. He told the four men who were working the oars: "Pull like hell, boys!"

Joan watched the boat pull up on the sand, she heard it crush the pebbles and the shells. Ross jumped into the water and ran towards her, his eyes frantic with anxiety. He put his arms around the woman, and she made a nod of the head which meant: "Yes, he is gone." Then he felt himself holding in his arms the whole weight of Joan.

The men stayed over near the boat, dumbfounded, fearing to have understood that this place, so full of happiness a month before, had turned into a graveyard. Even the dog was no longer there to welcome them with his joyful barking. One of them noticed a cross, another saw a second one; under the burning sun the men removed their caps. They looked with curiosity at the black whaleboat; they understood even less; but they had a premonition of a hideous drama.

Ross, supporting Joan, led her slowly over to the cabin. Bare-headed, the captain stopped in front of the small mound bordered with coral. She said simply: "Jock is there, with Wolf." They continued on, and when they arrived in front of the second cross, she said in the same blank voice: "The escapee from Noumea; he killed Jock, he killed Wolf. I am the one who killed him."

The captain endeavoured to piece together the elements of the drama, he resolved not to ask any more questions for now. He let the young woman cry on his shoulder, spoke to her of "Dad" and MacGillie, both of them impatient to see them ... her again.

He felt how difficult it was to take on the role of comforter; he carried on with it for the whole length of the beach, after summoning the men who had unloaded a prepared meal.

She watched the sailors approaching with an embarrassed look, she went over to them and held out her hand, to show them that she had understood their sympathy and that she thanked them for it.

They agreed not to weigh anchor until the next day; Ross spent a part of the evening with Joan, he explained to her that he was obliged to draw up on the spot a statement of all that had happened. He wrote down what she dictated, and went back on board the yacht, respecting the wish that she had expressed to spend her final night on the island.

Early the next morning, Ross and two of his men examined the scene of the drama, took notes, measured up the whaleboat, and inspected Louis' hut without finding anything; the only pieces of evidence of the escapee's existence were his straw hat, his pistol containing the case of a recently fired cartridge, and the boat.

The small cabin was dismantled in twenty minutes, and the men took two trips to transport everything that had made up the camp site. Soon all that was left were a few traces showing that humans had been present on the small deserted island. On the creek, a weir that sang night and day; on the beach the dismal whaleboat that had washed up like some vile thing. Between the two, one cross, then another.

At the second hoot of the siren, Joan was still busy placing green palm fronds on Jock's tomb; at the third one, she felt herself weaken, she would have preferred to die right there and disappear into the sand to be with her dead lover.

She took a grip on herself; unable to utter a sound, her lips shaped the words: *Good bye, my Jock*; then she felt that she also owed an adieu to the faithful dog who slept with his master: her lips trembled and tried to say: *Wolf, good bye.*

Then she walked down the sandy slope to the eternally singing beach, towards the eternally blue sea, and climbed aboard the launch.

In her cabin on the yacht, Joan thought constantly about arriving in Sydney; she sailed over a dark ocean, one side of which she was just leaving, and preparing herself to land on the other shore, where the sadness of two men and the renewal of her own grief were waiting for her. She was on the poop deck when the *Matano* sailed through the heads and entered Sydney Harbour. Its numerous coves planted with greenery, the red slopes of roof tiles gleaming in the sun, all had the same old cheerfulness. The small sailboats swept by like albatrosses, the double-prowed ferries were still crossing back and forth, laden with people fleeing the narrow, noisy streets of the city.

By the time the *Matano* was moored at the dock, Joan saw with a certain relief that her father and Jock's father already knew; Ross had been able to get a message to them a few minutes before. Joan was calmer than she had ever been, and it was she who, after the silent kisses of greeting, helped to support the two men, clasping them in her arms as they walked away.

Soon afterwards, she found herself in the garden beside the harbour; there the dear departed poured salt on her wounds. Jock was everywhere, following her like her shadow. But she was brave enough for three. MacGillie had taken the blow without a word; at first he had not wanted to believe the pencilled note that Ross had passed on to him. The doctor, even though he had handled suffering in all its forms, could not resign himself either. He could not comprehend how Joan had been able to withstand it, why her mind had not snapped like the string of a bow stretched too far. He kept an eye on her, gave her everything that might relax the grip of her suffering and restore her former strength.

One day, he surprised his daughter in the garden while she was stitching together some tiny items of clothing. He kissed her and thought he could see a glimmer of happiness cross over their threshold.

That night, between two pipes, Kirving said to Old Mac: "She is safe and sound: one of these days, you and me, we're going to be grandfathers!"

TEN

Joan is reading in the shade of a tall mimosa, while Donald Jock MacGillie, aged three, is towing a sailboat which is making heavy way on a sea of buffalo grass.

Suddenly she gets up, so suddenly as to make her book drop onto the lawn. She looks out at the harbour, her eyes strangely fixed on a ship sailing by several cable lengths offshore from the terrace. Joan has recognised the funnel and flag of the Dutch Shipping Company; it is the *Van Spilbergen* on its way to Java … via the Great Barrier Reef.

When the vessel had disappeared, she closed her eyes to follow it all the better, and the silver wake parting the blue water carried her far, far away to the North. Just at that moment, the breeze which had arisen rustled the tattered leaves of the banana trees, wafting to her the fragrance of the corals yielding up the previous night's dew to the sun.

Joan would have preferred to stand there, eyes closed; but two fat tears forced her to open her eyelids. Donald was clinging to her dress, he wanted to see, too. But she could not show him what she was seeing from afar. So she picked up the child and smothered him with kisses.

www.ingramcontent.com/pod-product-compliance
Lightning Source LLC
Chambersburg PA
CBHW031209260626
47169CB00004B/1294